WOMB CHILD

WOMB CHILD

Alethea Pascascio

Queen Publications

WOMB CHILD

ISBN: 0-9778377-3-4
        978-0-9778377-3-1
First Printing May 2008
LCCN: 2007939442

Printed in the United States of America

Queen Publications' Paperbacks are published by Queen Publications,
P.O. Box 496, Antioch, IL 60002.

10 9 8 7 6 5 4 3 2 1

PUBLISHER'S NOTE:

Acknowledgements

I give all praises and glory to God for dropping the seed of this story into my spirit. Thank you for opening my eyes and expanding my mind.

To my parents- Ray and Margaret Sherls. Your love and support for this project and me has been unwavering. Thank you for not relinquishing or eradicating the gifts (children) God so graciously bestowed upon you. You always said we could do anything we wanted to do and become anyone we wanted to be. I believed it then and it has become apparent in my life now.

And to every person who can feel with every fiber of their being that there is much more to life than what they are currently experiencing- you're right. Pray and ask God to let everything that He's put on the inside of you manifest on the outside.

…Pursue your purpose, it could change a single life or save millions

What if Martin Luther King Jr. had not been born or allowed the vicissitudes of life to overtake him?   What about Ben Franklin?   What about Mother Theresa? What about the person you call your best friend? What about... you? —Would anyone know the difference?

"Before I formed you in the womb I knew you..."

- Jeremiah 1:5

WOMB CHILD

Queen Publications
Author Email Contact: Alethea@queenpublications.com
http://www.queenpublications.com

Chapter One

6 weeks

It all happened so fast. One minute I was listening to the final instructions for my journey then the next thing I knew I was competing against millions for a chance at life. Since I was already predestined to win, I'm not even sure why the others showed up. But now that I reflect on it, I know exactly why they were there. They, the multitude of sperm that raced against me, were similar to the type of people you see everyday. Some were 'haters' with ill-intentions, wanting nothing more than to take my place and wreak havoc on the earth. Others were my 'motivators', cheering me on and running interference for me against the opposition. And the rest were mere 'distractions' trying to throw me off course, but not necessarily to assist the 'haters'. No, they had their own agenda. The 'distracters' started out being in it to win it, but when the journey got rough they became too discouraged to continue and tried to put up road blocks to keep me back with them, especially when it became obvious that I was going to be the 1 out of 100 million- who triumphed.

This is my second time trying to give it a go. The first time I beat the system (at least I thought) and ended up where some one else should have been, but it didn't work out. My would-be mother miscarried me. I should have learned that your date is set in stone from the others who had returned after trying to sneak in. None, absolutely none, are born before their time.

So here I am sitting in this warm sac of fluid surrounded by sounds that I can't quite describe as noise. They are too familiar. Too soothing. They lull me to sleep. They awaken me. They make the darkness come alive. The thud of heartbeats, the whoosh of nutrients pumping through my lifeline- a cord connecting me to my mother, the rumbling of her stomach after she has eaten something spicy. I'm really going to miss this place.

Mom doesn't even know she is pregnant yet. Won't my parents be surprised to find out that the night of their one year anniversary was truly the beginning of a new life.

I know it all seems a little rushed but I couldn't take any chances. I was assigned to them from the beginning of time and had almost given up hope of getting them together. Talk about stubborn, there couldn't be any two people in the world more stubborn than my twenty-eight year old parents, Carrie and Donald Hillman.

It is not easy getting two people together at the right time and place. Then having them move beyond their issues, embrace true love, and start a family can be even harder.

I'd spent many years peering over the edge of Heaven

playing match-maker before my persistence finally paid off. Dad had run out of excuses for not taking a vacation and Mom stopped pinching pennies long enough to splurge on a much needed trip to Maui. The two of them locked eyes at the Kaanapali Shore Hotel's reservation desk and have been inseparable ever since.

Although many incidents happen, none are accidents- not even who your parents are. Everyone comes to earth this way but seem to forget the process by the time they are old enough to tell it. But not me. I plan on remembering and telling everything. Like when Mom decided to treat herself to the mink coat she had seen in a sales paper instead of taking a vacation.

Do you know how difficult it was to distract her from going to the store for an entire week? I had so many obstacles thrown in her path that by the time she was able to make her way to the store, the sale had ended. So off to Hawaii she went. I'd finally completed what I had hoped to be the last arduous task involving my parents.

Not that I'm against hard work, quite the contrary. Hard work can often build character. It's the idea of hard work being synonymous to struggling that I'm against. Why struggle so much with life when you're tapped into the source that has infinite wisdom? But the second your spirit enters that embryo your angelic abilities began to perish and the moment you're pushed out of the womb your memory starts to fade, both are because of the tainted environment. And years later, you end up just like everybody else- going in circles, knocking your head against the wall trying to rediscover your purpose. But no, not me. I have nine months to float around and do nothing but commit my assignment to memory. This really makes me wonder how everyone else spent their time when they were 'on the inside'.

Chapter 2

8 weeks

What a difference two weeks make.

Not only has Mama's cycle stopped but she's throwing up. At first she thought she had a touch of the flu but after considering all of her symptoms, she knew right away that there was a baby on the way.

"Donald," she yelled with excitement. "Donald," she called out to him again. "I think we are pregnant."

I could hear my Dad's faint response from somewhere in the distance. "What?"

Fluid sloshed around me as my little body was tossed to and fro from what felt like Mom jumping up and down. "Pregnant. I think we're pregnant."

Dad's voice came nearer. I could hear his disbelief, "Pregnant?"

For a moment time stood still when Mom stopped jumping. Then the two of them embraced, the warmth of it flooding through her body and over me in my dark home. It

15

would be months before I would lay eyes upon either of my parents again, but I basked in their happiness all the same.

After what felt like a happy eternity, the two split apart and the questioning began, those same questions I remembered from before, when I had tried to come to earth too early.

Those days had been filled with a sort of nervous energy, both from my excitement to be born and the eventual fear of having come too early. Though warned by others, eventually experience taught me the problem with departing for earth too soon. It was dangerous. More than dangerous, it went against the natural order of things. But none of that mattered now. The time and place I had been given since the beginning of time had finally arrived. Knowing this journey was authentic, I could relax. I felt at ease in my mother's belly, listening to the two of them ask each other incredulously whether I truly existed.

"Are you sure?" Dad asked, but I could tell he knew. There was too much pride in how he said it.

"As sure as one of these tests can be. Can you believe it?!" Mom jumped again, unable to withhold the excitement. "I have to call my mother and brother! Hmmm. I'll need to see Doctor Sprigg first."

In Heaven, we always used to gather and watch when a friend of ours was first announced to the world. When the first announcement of an imminent baby girl or baby boy left the lips of the new mother, we would watch in awe and smile for the happiness our angelic friend must feel in her womb. It was an event that, no matter how often it occurred, was cause for great celebration. I wondered how many of my friends above were doing the same for me right then.

Dad laughed, "Wow. I never thought I would be a father." He savored the last word, repeating it again, "Father... My mother's going to do backflips. She'll finally have that little grandchild she's been dreaming of..."

"Since you introduced me to her." Mom finished the sentence for him and they both started laughing again. "Oh, I hope it's a little girl. I've always wanted a daughter."

Dad made a noise and stifled a laugh.

"I guess you probably want a boy then?"

"I'll admit it. I've always wondered what it would be like to teach a little guy to throw the ball around or ride his bike."

"You can do all of that with a girl!" Mom said with enthusiasm. She was too happy to be annoyed with him.

"You have a point there. Well, you know what? I don't even care right now. We're pregnant! That's all that matters. You, my love, are having a baby."

I quaked in response to Mom's jubilance, knowing that I'd finally arrived at the right time. I wish I could say something to the angels above, send a message saying 'thank you for your friendship. This moment is everything we had always imagined it to be.'

Eventually the real questions came, the nitty gritty, and the logistics of it all. I thought fondly on how incredible it was that so much was being considered.

"Do you think we'll need a bigger house?"

"Oh, I don't know about that, Carrie. We just moved in here. I think the second room will work for a nursery."

"What if we have another child someday?"

"Well, then we'll have a problem. Let's go ahead and have this one first though."

Mom chuckled, "Yeah, I suppose we oughta take it one at a time."

"So, what is the plan then?"

"What do you mean?"

"We shouldn't call everyone just yet, right?"

"Why not? I can't wait to tell Mom."

"We should make sure first. Like you said, call Doctor Sprigg before anything else."

"I suppose. Oh, I just can't wait to get started. I can buy new curtains, the ones with the little teddy bears…or cartoon characters, that would be so cute."

"Shouldn't we know if it's a boy or a girl before we buy anything?"

"My goodness, Donald. You're such a downer." Mom commented with a slight laugh, making sure he knew she was joking.

"Hey, someone's gotta do it." Dad added.

"Yeah, usually it's me. Remember that next time you stop and stare at the big screen TVs."

"How did I know you would say that?"

The playful banter was exactly as I had witnessed months after they first met in Hawaii.

Their excitement was so palpable that I couldn't help but let it sweep over me. Maybe it was the rapid pattering of Mom's heart or the steady, powerful voice of my father, but everything was right in that moment, as right as I could have imagined it.

The first time in this position, I had felt nervous, a tingle in the back of my neck as I waited for something to go wrong. I had known somehow that things were not right. This time, I felt nothing of the sort. I knew that everything was alright because I felt serene. The bloom in my chest that had become a heart beat lightly. Gone was the dark veil that had immediately descended upon my first trip to earth.

My parents, however did not know any of this. They knew only that they were less than a year away from becoming parents for the first time. The only thing they knew was that in mom's belly was a new life and that they were responsible for bringing it into being. I wondered what that feeling could possibly be like. It must be incredible.

Chapter 3

8 and ½ Weeks

Their plan was simple. Both Mom and Dad had awaken at six AM that morning, prepared to visit Doctor Sprigg, a family friend and long time confidant. They would return before noon and begin telling Mom's family the news.

Unfortunately, the phone interrupted their plans. Mom had complained about it often in recent weeks constantly ringing. Dad usually became upset after it rang and soon I began complaining as well, silently in my fluid bed. So, when the phone sounded off that morning, I woke immediately, drawn by what I was sure would be a small argument.

"Donald! Your darn phone is ringing again."

He sighed deeply and stamped back toward the bed where the metallic ring was beginning to repeat. With a hasty, "Yes, sir" and the slam of the phone landing back on the heavy surface, the phone was silent.

Without a word passed between them, I could feel the

worry start dripping through Mom's veins as she jerked upright, pulling me with her. I was just getting used to the sensation of being tugged in whatever direction Mom decided to move. It was always surprising, but the soothing rhythmic pumping of her heart usually extinguished my uneasiness.

"Donald, no. Tell me that wasn't the office." Mom complained suddenly.

"Yes it was, Carrie. I have to go in. This account...it's just. I have to." He didn't finish the sentence but stalked away again, the door closing not very gently behind him.

"Donald! You told them, didn't you? You had to have told them? How could they call you in?" She was still pleading, but there was anger in her words now.

A muffled voice called back from beyond the closed door. "Of course I told them, Carrie. It's just, if I don't close this account before the weekend things could just get worse at the firm."

"Worse? What do you mean worse?"

"I just need to go. I'm sorry. Call Doctor Sprigg and try to reschedule for this afternoon. I promise I'll be back." Dad's voice was no longer muffled. He was back in the room and had moved close to Mom.   "I..I'll do what I can. Call me if anything happens?"

"Of course." And with that, Dad was scurrying around

22

for another two minutes before silence descended over the room.

Mom was crying now, and I knew it was not merely for the fact that she needed to reschedule a doctor's appointment. I wished only that I could comfort her myself.

***

It had been a long day thus far. Mom called Doctor Sprigg shortly after Dad left and changed the time of her appointment. Dad hadn't called and she would need to leave soon. They would be going at three o'clock that afternoon, and not too long ago Mom mumbled that it was one-thirty. The anxiety in her was nearly overwhelming as I struggled to relax myself and focus on my own thoughts, on my purpose in being there. *Listen to her heartbeat,* I told myself. *Just listen to the heartbeat.*

My home, warm and so close to her, vibrated with the energy coursing through her body, telling her and me that something important was about to happen, regardless of how upset she was. Against my will, I fell victim to the stress, unable to calm myself any more than the woman within whom I was growing. Every second, the drumming cadence of her heart echoed against my head, almost interpreting what was going through her mind – the developing annoyance, excitement, and apprehension. Dad should be here with her right now and was not. The early morning phone call had taken care of that.

Ironically or not, she had no idea what I knew. I had the blueprints in my mind – I had been trained and drilled on exactly what would happen to me when I arrived here yet she still made me nervous.

After all, I was a surprise to her that was even greater than the lottery and the shock had just begun to set in. It made it that much harder with Dad absent. The most I could hope to do was remain happy and hope she felt it. Unfortunately, Mom's emotional state often dominated both of us.

Mom started talking rather loudly to herself, growing angrier with Dad for his lateness. "I should have demanded him not to go…it's getting so late… I can't believe he'd make me go alone."

Her uneasiness was upsetting, but so was a concern much more subtle than a simple disagreement between my parents. I had been on earth before and knew the emotions expecting couples went through. I have also felt the sheer apprehension of knowing I had deviated from the natural order of things. That alone, left me waiting on a daily basis for something to go wrong. Now here I am again, but this time at the right place and time, yet only one day after they learned of my existence, still something went wrong. I willed myself not to think of it, but it was hard, too hard.

WOMB CHILD

As the hour got later, my imagination grew wilder. There were too many possibilities and I had seen each of them while in Heaven. Yet, I knew I needed to remain positive, for Mom's sake.

I desired a break from it all, so I turned to a story I remembered hearing while still above, in Heaven. The angel who had told me was wiser than he appeared, having spent generations waiting and planning to return below. I took much of what I learned from that angel. His confidence was infectious as he waited for the right moment to depart. His story of failure was different from my own though. I would come to know him as Jeremiah.

When he was sent below the first time, his was a perfect union. His life was destined to be one of true greatness, a man the world had longed for a long time. I never saw him depart the first time. I had not yet met Jeremiah and only know of his experiences through stories he told. But, his stories were engrossing.

Destined for birth to two doctors married in Lancaster, California, Jeremiah had done much the same as I had. He maneuvered, created happy incidents, and ensured that his mother and father would meet and fall in love. Such is our role before leaving. After years of poking and prodding his would be parents, he finally left Heaven for what was supposed to be an incredibly important life- to cure AIDS.

For five months he basked in the glow of excitement and the energy his parents displayed, waiting for his time to shine, to be born and join the world and embark on a journey to greatness.

It was with a sad heart and very few details that Jeremiah described his final week on Earth. For some reason, if I asked him about his parents he would gush for days on end, but a single mention of what had brought him back above would silence him indefinitely, unwilling to describe what had prevented his imminent birth.

"Two-fifteen. Where is he?" Mom's frantic voice returned my mind to events at hand. I also started wondering why Dad was so late. Why would he leave Mom waiting and prolong the joyful revelation of a baby on the way. He would be so happy.

The phone eventually rang. I willed her to answer it, hoping Dad was calling to say he was on the way home. Mom ignored the call. Her mood had turned cold, almost chilling, spreading from my belly to my head. She walked the floor for a few minutes before bolting out of the house. The distrust and anger I could feel breeding inside of her was discomforting to me. An upsurge of nausea fluttered in my belly, a sensation I did not like at all.

The next hour was quiet and very bumpy. Mom had driven many times before through the streets of Northern

Chicago, but rarely could I recall an instance in which I had been so honed in on the undulating up and down motion I was currently stuck in. Maybe I was focused on the car's every rock and turn because there were no other sounds, no response from the outside world to my silent inquiries. Not even a simple song playing on the radio.

I knew where we were going, yet I wanted to know more. When the car finally stopped, my liquid fortification began to settle. Eventually the sounds of honking cars echoed around me, the mechanical symphony of the city which I had heard only twice before when Dad had taken Mom out for the evening. It was an odd experience, the kind I could not grow accustomed to, kind of annoying actually.

The noise soon died down, victim to Mom's quick pace and the thankfully less strident confines of the Doctor's office she had slipped into. While settling down my internal ears honed in on the sound of my fellow peers. There were so many!

All around me echoed the voices of a dozen or more other angels from Heaven; they were fetuses as well, waiting for their time to be born. It had been over two months since I heard a single voice other than Mom's and Dad's that I could identify with, so this was a pleasant surprise.

In truth, the voices were greatly muffled, hidden away behind layers of clothing and their soon to be mothers, but if there is a single thing I or any other child yet unborn can do, it is listen. And as I listened, I made out the echo of at least a half dozen conversations on the fetus frequency.

"She eats the worst things...pickles and waffles....sauerkraut and lemon."

"Only another month! I cannot believe it's almost time for..."

"...tomorrow. They haven't told anyone yet."

"Did we meet up above? I'm almost positive I know you from above."

The voices went on and on, sharing tales of intrigue from within their shallow cocoons and I yearned to speak with them, to hear more of their experiences and expectations. Mom never closed the gap between us though. She stopped only for a moment to speak with a woman who had a slow way of talking, "Can I help you?"

"Hi. It's Carrie Hillman. I'm here to see Doctor Sprigg."

"Ah, yes. Mrs. Hillman. Good thing too. You almost didn't make it on time. Would have had to reschedule. Please fill out the first few questions on this form."

I could feel the muscles tighten in Mom's stomach as her ink pen quickly scratched in answers on the paper. "Glad I made it on time. My husband's boss called him in. I'm sure you know how it can be sometimes."

"Yeah. Unfortunately. You can actually go on and head back to the last room on the left. He should be able to get you in right about now. There should also be a nurse in there to direct you further."

The shuffling of feet and lurch of forward movement told me Mom was making her way to the room where Doctor Sprigg would see her. Despite the sickening lump of acidic discomfort that had settled down on top of me, somewhere in the midst of Mom's belly, I remained excited. Not only had I heard the siren song of a dozen others about to be born just like me, but it was finally time for Mom to know I was truly coming.

"Please, put this gown on. Doctor Sprigg will be in shortly." An unfamiliar voice said.

"Thank you."

A few more minutes passed before I felt Mom finally stop moving and settle down, her body slowly releasing bits of the tension she had felt for hours. When the door creaked open, she tensed up yet again, her mind clearly focused on a point far from that room. I felt a pang of worry for her but let it subside as I knew the Doctor's news would cheer her up.

"Ah, Mrs. Hillman. How are we doing today?" His voice was springy, reminding me for some reason of the ride in Mom's car. I practically rose and fell with each syllable he spoke.

"Good. And you, Doctor?"

"Wonderful. Just wonderful. So, you believe you're expecting, is that correct?" I could hear the verbal nudge in his words. He actually sounded more excited than she was.

"Haha," she laughed feebly. "Yes. I took one of those home tests and it came back positive. So… here I am. Thought I should make sure."

"Ah yes. Absolutely! Well, we're just going to do a couple of quick tests and take a look to make sure and you can be on your way."

"Thank you, Doctor."

"That's what I'm here for." He said it playfully and Mom laughed again, a beautiful sound.

I strained to hear more, wanting to know what was happening outside, but could only wait.

The room was oddly quiet as the Doctor bustled about, telling Mom to hold this or do that. I didn't care much for the process, only the outcome. I was ready.

But no sooner than Dr. Sprigg had entered and laughed away her nervousness, he sat down and told her, "It's rather late in the day Carrie, so it will probably take a day to get back the lab results."

A day? I didn't like the sound of that at all.

"Can't you just check on a machine, ultrasound or something?"

"Honestly, I try not to do ultrasounds unless they are absolutely necessary, such as when I suspect there is a problem. The basic lab tests we've already done are sufficient. We don't really need to do anything else."

I bellowed from my silent home inside of her to demand an ultrasound, but moments later she responded, "Alright doctor. I suppose I can wait another day."

"Beautiful. Just make sure your contact information is up to date with Susan and I'll give you a call tomorrow afternoon."

She sighed and started standing up.

"And Carrie."

"Yes, Doctor?"

"Those home tests rarely give a false positive... Congratulations."

Musing that the doctor was not such a bad fellow after all, I basked in the knowledge that in a day my Mom and Dad would know for sure I was on the way.

When we passed through the waiting room I further announced my pending arrival by shouting over the din of voices still chatting. "I'll probably see some of you in a few months!"

Chapter 4

8 and ½ Weeks

I didn't notice the bouncing motion of the ride on the way home. I was too excited by the prospects that lay ahead of me. I had always known that when this time came, the experience would be incredible, but had no idea how happy I would truly be. I knew Mom had to feel it as well. The rapid pitter patter of her heart and the gentle hum of a tune she droned as we arrived home gave more tranquility than any pacifier ever could.

By the time, Mom made it into the bedroom and flopped down on the bed, I was so sleepy. I felt a stillness rush over my body as she rubbed her stomach and shooshed me and herself to sleep. The darkness descended over us both and dreams took hold. As usual, thoughts and visions of Jeremiah came to mind.

Jeremiah was never angry about his return to Heaven yet he wouldn't divulge the circumstances surrounding it. But his failed voyage didn't stop him from offering advice to any of us waiting for our time to come. As one of the few Returners who left at the right time and was forced back, he was the least upset and the freest with his advice, if only we did not ask about *why* he returned.

It must have been a horrible feeling for him though, knowing that his time had passed and the goals and purpose God had given him were not being achieved below. I'm sure it was a horrific experience and yet he remained silent about it, always working, always pulling the strings that would one day bring him back to Earth. I had spent hours talking to him, watching him work.

"You cannot simply push them toward each other," he used to say constantly, "you must create a situation in which they can *find* each other. This is the hardest part."

I would ask him how you help two people *find* each other without pushing them together.

"What you must learn more than anything are the subtleties of life." He often spoke in parables, emulating the methods of our Father.

"Your mother and father may be young, brash and temperamental. However, a tense bridge will hold the weight of a hummingbird without bending. That same bridge will snap beneath the weight of an elephant. Yet with time and reinforcement, the bridge will hold anything."

The image always stayed with me. The need for patience was paramount. Again and again Jeremiah showed his patience, maneuvering his new mother and father for ages, three full generations beyond his previous journey.

I was there beside him when he distracted a man from a coffee stand with a gentle breeze and a dandelion seed so he could witness a young woman in dangerously high heels trip and spill her armload of books to the ground. When the man helped her up, their eyes locked for 10 seconds or so, relating a connection, a deeper spark, what some might call love at first sight. One thing led to another and they ended up going out on a date that lasted several hours.

From there, Jeremiah's work was finished for a long while. The two were finally together and though Jeremiah watched hawkishly, he did very little to influence their relationship. He knew their romance had entered an orbit of its own and would flourish without his intervention. And he was right. We watched their love develop into something akin to those fanciful fairy tales children begged their mothers and fathers to read.

On occasion, when no angels were departing, we would observe Jeremiah's would-be grandparents sitting quietly at the window table in an elegant restaurant or on a sofa, enjoying each other's company. It was comforting and at the same time exciting to think of our own futures and families sitting comfortably together, merely enjoying each other's companionship.

WOMB CHILD

The pair was married in less than two years and Jeremiah was able to start plotting the next step in his elaborate plan. For, a child had already been destined for the happy couple on their sofa – her name was Susan. She had spent a lot of her time in solitary preparing for her travel and allowed Jeremiah to set her stage. After all, she would one day become his mother.

And so, twenty-six years after the first meeting of her parents, Susan stumbled into a library on a particularly gloomy Monday morning looking for a book to salvage a soon to be overdue Social Science paper. Her eyes fell heavily upon a particular man in mahogany-corduroy slacks stacking books behind the desk absent-mindedly. The man's name was Peter and this was the exact moment Jeremiah had been waiting for.

A master in his craft, Jeremiah tripped up the sleepy-eyed library assistant on an errant shoelace and sent him stumbling into the stack of books. Landing heavily on a pile of recently returned Social Science journals, Peter was soon helped to his feet by the procrastinating young woman. Susan asked for his assistance, Peter offered her a handful of journals and the rest was what Jeremiah liked to call family history.

Jeremiah's work would not be finished for years to come though. Peter and Susan had a flighty romance, full of clashes between families, mindsets and moral beliefs. On a weekly basis, one or the other would stamp into the night angrily, unwilling to apologize for a misspoken word. Jeremiah would be there each time, concentrating with every ounce of energy he had. He even convinced ex-boyfriends and ex-girlfriends to take jobs out of state, and manipulated major events to make both young lovers look favorable to the other's parents.

Jeremiah always said, "Nothing in life is easy. There are hardships and there are weaknesses. These are human nature. What you must help them realize is that some things are more important than any disagreement or temporary hardship. You must help them move past the petty little things like jealousy or their family's disapproval. Love is much more important."

I clung to those words from Jeremiah vehemently, holding them close to my heart, knowing that I would remember them afterwards and use them to be the man I was chosen to become.

The comforting words of my dear friend faded gradually as I was slowly awaken by the sound of a man whispering gently. Dad was home and apologizing, waking Mom- asking her forgiveness for not being there.

"I love you. I promise I will be there next time, no matter what."

"I know that you will." Her voice was quiet, though warm. The anger I had felt from her earlier was not there anymore. It had completely faded and I delighted in the tender warmth of her love for my father. "I love you too, Donald."

With that, Dad placed a heavy hand upon her belly and spoke softly, "I will be there, for both of you."

"I know, Donald. I know."

***

The next morning, I was once again jostling to and fro in my mother's belly, tossed about by her constant pacing, while we both waited for the fateful sound of the telephone.

While yesterday's pacing had been full of impatience and anger, today's was a simple case of suppressed jubilance. Mom and Dad were waiting for *the* call so they could celebrate properly, tell the family, start picking out cribs and baby clothes. That call would make everything official.

The day dragged on. As I waited impatiently for my mother and father to celebrate, I began to wonder if the phone would ever ring. Eventually, my parents started discussing what was supposed to be Dad's golf outing, a weekly occurrence that he was willingly skipping to wait for the call with Mom.

"Carrie, I want to be here. I promised I would be here."

"Donald. The phone might not ring for hours yet. It is still eleven o'clock. You should go and play golf. It is Saturday after all."

"You know I can't do that to you."

Mom laughed and playfully responded, "you can and you will! I've made up my mind. Now go."

Dad huffed and puffed a couple more times but was clearly in the process of complying with Mom's orders. His footsteps echoed upstairs along with the crash and clang of metal on metal.

Moments later his voice returned, "Okay. I'm leaving. But, when you get the phone call, I want to know immediately. Call me right away. I can't wait to tell the guys."

Mom stopped her pacing finally and settled down to what I assume was a television – rapidly changing voices and suggestions to buy different cleaning materials, new cars, and spicy tortilla chips echoed in my tiny space. The voices continued for what must have been hours when finally the rattling soprano of the kitchen telephone reverberated. Mom and I bounded for the kitchen.

"Hello?!

"Oh. Hi, Mr….

"No, he's not here right now.

"Yes, golfing with his friends.

"I'm sorry, sir... What do you mean?

"You can't mean to…I'll have him call you immediately.

"No. You must speak with him. I can't tell him this," Mom insisted.

"Hello?"

Something was wrong. Mom's heart started thumping rapidly and the happiness I had expected to overwhelm her had not arrived. In its place was a seething pool of something sticky, a very miserable feeling, akin to falling down backward and hitting one's head. Who had she just spoken to?

Only seconds later, I heard Mom dial a number and talk once again on the phone.

"Donald? It's me. You should come home.

"No, I don't know quite yet. But, I would really appreciate it if you came home now." There was no anger in her voice, only a soft pleading, begging Dad to return as quickly as possible.

"Thanks, hun. I love you, too." She hung up the receiver and returned us to the television, still blaring away about some or another amazing new, super fantastic cleaning compound that would remove any stain, even grass.

Mom suddenly silenced the television and together we sat, each contemplating our own worries. She was surely repeating the phone message over again in her mind while I waited for a different call to come, a happier call, *the* happier call.

Ultimately that call did come, maybe twenty minutes, maybe an hour later. It didn't matter what time, because it was almost ignored. The phone rang a half dozen times before Mom rose from her seat and picked up the receiver.

"Hello?

"Oh, hi Doctor Sprigg." Mom's voice, solemn.

"Yes? That is good news. Thank you very much.

"You have a wonderful weekend as well. I will see you very soon I imagine."

There was no elated response, no happiness, no jumping up and down as she had done four days beforehand. She simply sat back down to wait for Dad. I let her weariness descend over me allowing the reality to set in – she was not excited.

Chapter 5

8 and ½ Weeks

Dad returned quickly, with a happy sort of ring to his voice, awaiting the good news he assumed Mom had ready for him. "Carrie? Oh, what a day Carrie. I shot six over in the first round. Can you believe that?"

When she didn't answer immediately, I heard him step into the room, his voice still jovial. "Did you get the call? You got the call, right?"

"Yeah. I got the call." She hesitated for a moment before continuing, "Donald, your boss called."

"Hank Hartzman? What did that old fart want?" He said it playfully as though the tone of Mom's voice hadn't quite registered.

"He gave me a message for you." Mom paused briefly then continued, "the Brown account fell through. Someone has to take the heat for it. Donald, I think they've let you go."

Dad fell silent for a moment. I strained for any kind of sound. It was as though he had completely disappeared.

Finally he spoke, now softly and ignoring Mom's latter statement, "What did Doctor Sprigg say?"

"Donald, you've been fired." Her voice higher now, almost urgent.

Dad slipped back into silent.

Mom relented and answered his question. "Doctor Sprigg confirmed it. We are pregnant. He said I'm almost nine weeks along."

"Pregnant." Dad said it evenly, probably to himself then fell silent for a few seconds longer. Mom did not say anything either. I could imagine the two of them sitting in silence watching, trying to read each other's thoughts. My blindness to the world left me in speculation, wildly postulating what they could be thinking. There was no celebration though, it was all rather subdued.

Finally, as if the volume had been turned back up on a muted radio receiver, Dad spoke up, "You're pregnant!"

"Yep, over two months now."

"Wow. I can't believe it. This is something we always hoped for...and now." His excitement, however short-lived had filled my heart. He was thrilled about me. I knew Mom was too. I could feel it. But, that happiness was indeed fleeting as the cold hard facts of the first phone call settled upon them.

"Donald, we'll be okay." Mom said it almost as a

question, confidently but not purposefully. She was upset, nervous, and excited all at once and every bit of her relayed that. Her heart pounded faster, her breathing was rapid, and the rush and echo of emotion pulsing through me was as confusing as any experience I could ever experience on Earth.

Filled to the brim and on the verge of bursting, Mom could hardly contain her conflicting emotions and yet when she spoke, her slow, steady voice sounded absolutely at ease, supportive for her husband. "Donald. This is not as bad as it seems. Call Mr. Hartzman and talk to him. I'm sure he'll tell you this is not anything personal. You did an amazing job there and they all know it. This is just politics."

"Yeah, I suppose I did. But a baby, Carrie. Wow." He was obviously still in shock from the opposing emotions, unsure which was more appropriate at that moment.

"It's going to be okay. We have months until the baby comes. You and I both know you'll have a new job in no time. Consider talking to my brother. He'll help you out."

"I don't want to call your brother, Carrie." He said it absent-mindedly, clearly repeating a line he'd repeated numerous times in the past.

"He can help you. If you need his help, call him."

"I'll order something for dinner. I don't think either of us is in the mood to cook right now. Then I'm going to go call

Hank."

Finally, Dad moved, the heavy drops of his feet on the tile in the kitchen reverberated back to Mom and me beside the television. I tried hard to hear what he might be saying on the phone, but the distance was too great and Mom had turned the television back on. I got the impression she did not want to hear that phone call.

For what seemed like an eternity, Dad was gone, likely still on the phone arguing for his livelihood. Mom sat silently, rubbing her belly and humming tenderly to me. Her melodious tune was intoxicating. I could have listened to her forever but I knew it was only intermission for the drama unfolding in their lives. Nevertheless, we both waited patiently for a word from Dad, for any sign of good news.

The Chinese food delivery man had come and gone yet Dad was still on the telephone. Mom, possibly tired of being in suspense, quietly made her way into the kitchen. Just as suspected, Dad was still on the phone.

"Hank, this is incredible. No, I know how important the Brown account was....

"You think I don't know that. I worked my tail off for that account. Give me a break, my wife and I are going to have a baby!

"Yes, we just found out.

WOMB CHILD

"Oh, why thank you for your kind wishes. That really means a lot coming from a man who just laid me off for his own mistakes.

"No, Hank, I don't think you understand what I'm going through. This is ridiculous. Don't think I won't take this up with one of the partners." The vexation in Dad's voice was frightening. I had not heard either of my parents talk like that before and it was not a pleasant experience.

"Yeah, bye." The crack of the phone being roughly returned to its holster was jarring.

"The food's here." Mom spoke softly.

"Oh, hi hun. Sorry about that." The kindness had returned to his voice.

"I take it things didn't go well on the phone."

"Coward took 20 minutes to answer the call and then had the nerve to tell me that it wasn't personal. It was some kind of corporate politics. I say it's low-down, really. I poured my heart into that place. I missed your appointment yesterday to finalize the deal. How is it *my* fault? I brought the client to the table and got him to pick up his silverware, it was Hartzman's job to make him eat. That man couldn't manage himself out from underneath a wet paper towel." Dad sighed loud enough to awaken the dead.

"It's going to be okay, Donald. Like he said, this isn't your fault. This is corporate politics and you got caught in the

45

crossfire."

"I just…I just can't believe they would do this to me. So much of my life has gone into that place. It's the best firm in Illinois and I was one of their best brokers."

"That's right, babe. You were one of their best brokers and you'll get another job in no time. This is just a small bump in the road and you know it. Now come on. Let's eat this food before it gets cold."

With another deep sigh, I felt Dad hug Mom fiercely. Pressed between my parents, I felt a surge of exquisite joy, a raw and powerful love that eclipsed everything else. My parents would be okay. I would be okay. I didn't have an inkling of why the Brown account was so important. All I knew was that my parents were in love and that I, their son, was lucky to be cuddled between them at that moment.

The rest of the evening was spent discussing finances and possible job opportunities. As much as I desired to hear them discussing me and our future, they were clearly preoccupied with the material repercussions of my imminent arrival.

"How much do we have in savings?"

"Three, four months at least."

"Is that going to be enough?"

"It won't take that long for you to find another job. You'll have firms clamoring for you as soon as you send out resumes."

Dad laughed, possibly lightening up under the strain of his new found unemployment. "That's all fine and good. But, we need to be sure we are alright. There's a baby on the way."

"We have months until we need to worry about the baby." My heart shrank a little at that statement. I knew it was not in malice or indifference. They were prioritizing and had not yet begun to think of me as their number one concern. It still hurt nonetheless.

"But the insurance, it's only going to remain active for sixty days," Dad informed. "Although, we don't need clothes or diapers yet, eventually you'll need to see Doctor Sprigg every couple weeks or so."

"We're fine for now, honey. My parents can help out if we absolutely need them to." And as though she had just remembered again, "And you should call my brother."

"Let's not go over this again, Carrie. You know the last thing I want to do is ask Jason for help. The man has never liked me."

"It doesn't matter if he likes you. He doesn't need to like you. But he'll help you because I'm his sister."

"Last resort. Jason is a last resort."

Mom sighed but let the topic go. "Alright. What's the first resort then? Where are we going to start?"

"I'm not sure. It's been a long time since I looked for a job. Smith, Jackson, and Silvan was through a college internship. Truth is, I've never really needed to look."

"Well, I did. First thing Monday morning we're going to sit down and write you up a new resume. Do you even have an old resume?"

"I suppose I do, but it is ten or twelve years old and lists the campus Dairy Queen as my last job."

"Okay then. So you don't have an old resume. Now we know step one. Tomorrow though, we're going to relax. We're going to forget about Hank Hartzman, Doctor Sprigg and my brother and just sit at home all day."

Dad chuckled, "I second that motion."

***

Two or three hours later, Mom left Dad to a rather raucous television program from which numerous explosions and a slew of unfamiliar and angry sounding words emanated. While he was occupied with that she started making phone calls. The first person she needed to call, as she had told Dad, was her mother.

"Hi Mom, it's Carrie.

"I'm doing wonderful. How are you doing tonight? Is Dad still watching that show?" She laughed knowingly, "Yeah,

Donald is too.

"Yeah, lots of explosions and profanity. He loves those things.

"Listen, Mom. I actually called for a reason tonight.

"No, it's good news. Very good news actually.

"I'm pregnant." Mom's subdued voice suddenly became much higher.

"I know! I just found out today.

"No, Mom. I'll tell Dad….okay, I'll hold on.

"Hi Dad. Yes…. I told Mom I wanted to tell you. About nine weeks... I visited the doctor yesterday.

"No Dad, I've never smoked.

"I don't like coffee. But thank you for being concerned.

"Dad, I don't own exercise tapes.

"O.K. sure I'll talk to Mom. Bye Dad. I love you too."

Mom was quiet for a little while then chimed in again. "Was he like that about me and Jason?

Mom laughed at something Grandma had said. "Well, no… Things are actually a little bit hectic right now. Donald was laid off today from his job." The excitement now gone from her voice.

"I know. I'm doing my best to keep his spirits up. He's pretty down about it and with the baby coming now, we're going to be very tight on money if he doesn't get a job soon. I've tried to convince him to call Jason.

"I know they don't like each other. I don't really care though. I don't like this at all. Donald's never needed to look for work before. He graduated from college and had a job lined up for him through a recommendation from a firm he interned at during his senior year. All he has is connections right now, and a termination notice from the only professional employment he's ever had.

"I just don't know… I hope so. The last thing I want is for this to become a stressful experience. We don't need that kind of stress weighing us down. Do me a favor, would you? Casually mention to Jason that I want to talk to him.

"No, I'll call him and tell him about the baby. I just want him to worry a little, maybe he'll feel a tiny bit of sympathy before I talk to him. God knows it might help.

"Alright Mom, well I've got to make a few more phone calls. So many friends and such big news.

"I love you, too. I'll talk to you really soon. Bye."

All of the sugar coated confidence I'd heard Mom offer Dad seemed to have been slightly forced. It didn't sound like she had the slightest confidence in his ability to land a new job right away. Oh how very interesting it was to hear Mom say one thing to Dad then articulate her true feelings to her mother.

That was the first time Mom's stance didn't affect me in

parallel. If fact, we were almost polar opposites on this issue. Her confidence was as solid as steel one minute and weak as straw the next, but mine did not waver.

Jeremiah would have only laughed at the predicament from above, carefully maneuvering pieces into place to solve Dad's employment issues and Mom's burden of stress. I wondered at that moment where Jeremiah was. He was surely still on Earth as well, an old man now no doubt, still living his life. I hoped that I might be able to meet him after I was born.

He wouldn't remember me, but then I wasn't entirely sure that I would remember him either.

Chapter 6

11 Weeks

Things change rapidly when adults are stressed out. Every crack of the heavy oak door against its metallic frame as Dad leaves in the morning and every biting remark from Mom only serve as reminders of their stress.

About a week ago Mom started eating less and the interactions between her and Dad became increasingly casual. They only spoke of the weather, the neighbors, the dog across the street. I didn't hear a single mention of myself and only the occasional mention of Dad's daily job searches.

Unfortunately, when two people take every precaution to ignore a painful reality, things will start to boil over. I waited patiently for something to happen, but soon it became apparent that waiting was the problem. So, I stopped waiting and started thinking; what could I do to reignite their spark, to make them realize that they should do everything in their power to be happy.

It wasn't that I had forgotten my place in Mom's womb or my silent position for the next six and a half months. I knew there was little I could do, but I was sent with a purpose. I was a diplomat, a talker, an important figure in the future of an entire region of the world. Surely, there was something I could do to appease my parents if no one else could.

One Saturday morning, I became fed up with the distance growing between my parents. I was far from willing to sit silently by any longer in the vacuum of protection that kept me from voicing my worries. Already bothered by Mom's meager diet, I did my best to upset her stomach a hair further. I twisted and writhed, somersaulted and flipped in the best imitation of a prenatal gymnast. What more could I do?

"Donald, where are you ?" Mom almost whispered his name the second time. "Donald."

"Yeah hun, what's wrong?" Dad's muffled voice dripped from above.

"Can you come here please?"

"Uh, sure. Hold on a minute."

"Hurry up."

The worry in her voice must have touched him as his voice grew stronger in a matter of seconds, "What's wrong Carrie?"

"I don't feel well." Mom's voice weak. I stopped moving, worried that I might have done too much, might have hurt her.

Dad's voice was strained now as he forgot that he was

avoiding his wife, "What's wrong?"

"I'm not sure. My stomach…it really hurts."

The two were silent for a moment as I considered what I might have just done.

"You're a little warm. You're running a small fever. I'm going to call Doctor Sprigg."

"Donald, it's Saturday. He's at home."

"I know, but maybe he'll know what's wrong. You haven't been back since the tests."

"I don't need to go back for another week, Donald. I'm only eleven weeks."

"Well, I think your body is telling us otherwise. I'll be back in a minute."

Mom moaned and lightly kneaded her belly as the muffled sound of Dad's voice on the telephone carried from the other room.

I hadn't considered that I might make Mom really sick. I just wanted to repair the rift that had come between them by making her uncomfortable enough to summon Dad for a little consolation. My plan could still work, if only for one day, if only for an hour.

A few minutes later, Dad's voice returned to the room, slightly happier, revealing what he found to be good news. "Doctor Sprigg says it is nothing to worry about just yet. The fever is minimal and happens on occasion. As for your stomach, you probably need to eat and get some rest."

"I figured…"

"And *if* you still don't feel well in a couple hours, we're to call him back immediately."

"You know we can't afford any extra medical bills."

"If you need the doctor, we're going. I'm much more concerned about your health than the bill." Dad spoke sharply, inviting no argument from Mom on the issue.

"Thank you, Donald."

The rest of the day, Mom and Dad kept each other company, laughing and conversing as if they were on their first date. The mellow steady drumming and gentle guitar strums of a wonderful blues singer played almost inaudibly in the background. I remained still, embarrassed by my tantrum and feeling guilty for Mom's discomfort yet even guiltier for having not caused it sooner.

The ploy had worked, bringing the two together after many days of silence. Unfortunately, they still did not mention me or the growing discontentment they both felt for Dad's unemployment. It would be another week before they turned to those uncomfortable topics.

And so, upset that I had yet to be mentioned, I started to reflect again on my life before being here. It consoled me in those weeks to think of the last words Jeremiah said to me before he departed for his second stint on Earth. It had been three decades since his first failed descent and the years had made him wiser than most in matters related to parents and their fickle nature.

"When you meet your parents for the first time, the moment is almost impossible to forget," he said it sadly but with a smile, perhaps replaying a fond memory. "But don't let the promise of that moment fool you though. Even when the desire to experience that feeling entices you to leave early, ignore the urge. The reward of finally seeing your parents at the set time is worth the wait."

I remembered and made sure to carry those words with me, repeating them nearly as earnestly as the instructions God gave me for my journey. It was the last thing Jeremiah ever said to me and it was often hard to remember those words without recalling the times I had spent watching him from above.

At first, Jeremiah's new life was as planned. His parents, living a comfortable life in a small town, had finally settled and left many of their bickering, hot blooded tendencies behind. But, something seemed to change months after Jeremiah's conception.

His mother, Susan, had always been temperamental, but kindness had long since manifested as a part of her personality. The little things no longer got to her as they had when she was young. Sure, they still had the occasional argument about the

WOMB CHILD

toilet seat's position or socks strewn about, but what couple doesn't? Yet it was obvious that something had definitely changed for the worse.

No one questioned her short temper or odd requests while she lumbered about, seven months pregnant and as irate as she had ever been. And the motherly love that I had witnessed in so many others from above was not there. When Jeremiah was finally born, it was no surprise when his mother regarded him with a cold indifference that should have been reserved for tax collectors and insurance sales men. For whatever reason, she chose that moment to decide that her lifelong wish for motherhood had been overrated.

Jeremiah grew quickly, as only a boy like Jeremiah could, but his family life was maddeningly dysfunctional. It had not occurred to Jeremiah's father, Peter, that the enmity his wife held toward their son would extend to him. By the time Jeremiah's second birthday arrived, his parents had found just cause to dissolve their marriage, going their separate ways in a messy divorce.

Whether angry that her life was now forfeit to a child who needed her attention day and night or disillusioned by the temporary hormonal fluctuations, Susan never fell into the role of a loving mother. She spoke the reassuring words at his crib-side and rocked him to sleep when he was collicky, but constantly complained the rest of the time, never satisfied.

Motherhood took a toll on Susan, sifting her like wheat, separating her from herself and everyone else. When the courage to fight through her issues remained as elusive as a four-leave clover, she almost willingly gave Peter sole custody of Jeremiah.

He didn't take to the role of singe father well. Tragically, Susan's distaste for Jeremiah had also caused Peter to become cold and distant. He spent most of his days working, having very little spare time for Jeremiah and the parental duties Susan so willfully dropped in his lap. He could have easily altered his schedule, but why would he? Peter could barely stand the sight of his son and the look of despair in eyes that yearned for nothing, but pure genuine love.

Day by day, Peter became even more cold and distant than Susan. For Peter, Jeremiah was a reminder of the love he had many years before that was now completely lost. Selfishly, he would spend his days ignoring the only good thing in his life and remembering the worst.

Eventually, Jeremiah became the ward of his grandparents, a loving couple in the heartland of Georgia, an auto mechanic and a pastry chef.

For as long as I watched Jeremiah grow, he did not display a single sign of happiness. Quiet in school, detached from his parents, and spiteful towards the love his grandparents showed him- Jeremiah had retained none of the traits I remembered from him in Heaven. Three decades of Jeremiah's efforts in Heaven seemed nullified in three short years. I know it appeared as if a mistake had been made in the assignment of his parents, but that's not so. Every experience and circumstance has the ability to build character and/or teach a lesson that can help people achieve their highest potential and purpose.

The problem lies in it being much easier to stand still as a victim than forge ahead as a victor. People also tend to become lazy and settle for mediocrity instead of fighting to remember and reclaim their purpose. I always hoped Jeremiah would wake up and do the latter, but my hopes for him were not enough he had to have them for himself.

Even with all of my God-given knowledge, I was still becoming a little concerned about my own journey. The last thing I wanted to do was abuse my existence or abnormally use my life. Therefore, remembering my purpose no matter what I come against is essential.

The week since my tantrum, there was steady conversation between my parents, something I was proud to have facilitated. Unfortunately, the mood around the house had transitioned to the point of open hostility. Instead of ignoring each other, Mom and Dad were now snapping at each other and the stress, as before, was causing much discomfort for me as well.

I understood what it meant for a mother only eleven weeks pregnant to feel the effects of the progesterone coursing through her body and the strain it could often put on relationships. This was not that kind of stress. The type burrowing into Mom's body was emotional- the we have a baby on the way, when is Donald going to get a job, we are running out of money, kind.

And Dad, poor Dad, spent every day for weeks leaving early in the morning and returning late at night with very little to show for his endeavors. As a result, he had his own type of stress that was comparable to if not greater than Mom's. He had the-why can't I find a job, there's a baby on the way, we need more money, I have to take care of my family, kind.

Their routine continued for weeks on end. Every morning, Dad relayed his list of job leads to Mom excitedly, tripping over what could only be loose items on the floor in his excitement to be out of the house and back out there knocking on doors. And every night he returned with a sour note, angrily relaying the bad news and the failures of the day's search, asking Mom if she had seen anything on the computer that looked promising. It seemed Mom's response was colder every day, alternating between helpful and impatient. She wasn't a secretary and slowly took to letting him know that.

***

It was Wednesday night and Dad had been gone since

very early that morning. By the time Dad returned home, Mom had already eaten a large dinner of pot roast and broccoli crowns and was performing the familiar routine of scraping the food particles from the day's dishes with a crisp, scratchy rhythm. I could almost inherently tell what actions were being performed, they were becoming more and more familiar to me everyday.

I felt as though I was beginning to understand how it was that a blind man could stroll confidently down a sidewalk without accidentally walking into the street. Humanity has truly lost touch with the power of sound and just how much one can discern from the pitch of a single statement or the cadence of a repeated motion.

"Carrie, are you in here?"

Neither one of us had heard Dad come home. The dish Mom was scraping clean dropped into the empty sink. "Yeah. I'm in the kitchen."

Dad's voice grew louder, "Hey, hun. How was your day?" It wasn't a question really. It was a nightly routine and the thick, tired blanket of routine was growing dustier with each passing day.

"Good. I'm just cleaning up." Mom's voice was equally redundant, simply repeating the words that had been planted fifteen months ago after the wedding, now part of the familiarity of marriage. "No luck?"

"No." His answer, curt.

Though she did not reply, Mom tightened in response, annoyed by his tone.

"I just want to lie down." Dad said plainly.

"Donald, we need to talk."

"I really just want to lie down right now."

"Well, too bad," her voice raised. "It's been almost three weeks and we have barely talked about this. We need to talk."

"Carrie, I've had a rough day and the last thing I need right now is to talk about it." Dad was clearly annoyed by Mom's persistence and facing rejection during his job search.

"Excuse me? You've had a rough day?" Frustration bubbled up in Mom's voice as she lashed back. "You're not the only person in this house. If you haven't noticed, one of us is pregnant and it sure as heck isn't you."

"Carrie, come on. I know you're having a hard time. Don't think I don't know that. What do you think I'm doing out there? I'm trying to make sure we can afford to have that child."

"*Afford to have that child*? What's that supposed to mean?"

I asked the very same question silently from within.

Dad was quiet for a long moment. He sighed heavily once, then again before replying. "You and I both know how hard this is starting to become. The visit to Doctor Sprigg last week?

Even with the extension on my benefits; it cost us almost five hundred dollars. What are we going to do when the time comes to start buying furniture? What about cloths and diapers – everything else?" He trailed off, seemingly unsure of how to continue.

This was nonsense. I knew as well as both Mom and Dad that they would figure out a way to make things work. I had witnessed these two go through hardships for much of their adult lives and there was no way something as small as finances would hold them back now. I waited for Mom to rise to my defense, to declare Dad insane for second guessing their destiny.

Nothing came though and the silence stretched on. The bickering had ceased and for every second the silence lasted, I felt more betrayed by the parents I had brought together so carefully.

Finally, Mom spoke, "Donald, this isn't the conversation I wanted to have right now."

"It's one we're going to have to consider sooner or later." They lowered their voices, talking normally, almost cautiously.

"No, right now you need to worry about getting a job. I told you to call Jason. Did you do it?"

Dad heaved another sigh, "No, I haven't called your brother yet. I told you, he's a last resort."

"Alright then. How are the rest of your *resorts* faring? Do you have any good leads?"

"Carrie, it's not that simple. Things aren't so black and white out there."

"Don't tell me how the business world works, Donald." The heat in her voice had returned, "I worked for the largest law firm in the state before you even graduated college. And, I earned that job."

"Hey! What's that supposed to mean?"

"Nothing…just, I know how these things work. You and I both know that your references aren't panning out. Hartzman is making sure your name is plastered over every inch of bad news related to that Brown account and the other firms are seeing that. If nothing pops up soon, you need to call my brother."

"Ugh, I just…I can't stand the thought of asking him for help."

"I don't care, Donald. You have a child on the way. *We* have a child on the way and we both know that Jason will do what he can to help us out."

"What if he doesn't?"

"What do you mean?"

"I mean, what if Jason can't help me. What then? That's the last road, right? After Jason, we're stuck up a creek and you're still pregnant."

"Is that what you're worried about? If he says no?"

"Maybe I am. A little bit. He doesn't run the company, Carrie. He's a Project Manager. Everyone's a Project Manager. What if he can't help? How are we going to pay for everything?"

"Well, I know after we married, we agreed that I'd come out of the workforce, but now-"

"No, Carrie," Dad cut in, obviously insulted by her suggestion. "Let me be the man I promised I would be. I'm going to take care of you, not the other way around. And not to belittle your skills, but I don't think a Legal Secretary's check can take care of our expenses, anyway."

The temperature on the inside felt like it went up about five degrees. Mom was definitely inflamed. "A Legal Secretary's check can keep our butts off of the street with a roof over your heads. How dare you pull that macho male chauvinistic mess at a time like this?"

"Okay, okay. I'm sorry." Dad' voice now a soft whimper. "I'm so sorry. I never meant to… I just… It's not supposed to be like this. It's one thing to struggle together. It's another thing to struggle with a child."

It was here that I realized what Dad was thinking. I had seen this before, the hesitation and the subtle hints. There was no malice or ill-intentions in Dad's voice. There was only fear, the kind of fear that I had seen a hundred times in the past.

Jeremiah had described it to me once as an irrational

response to responsibility. His own experience in dealing with this situation had preceded mine by decades but now I was starting to understand a small portion of what he must have gone through. The pain of realizing that one of my parents was about to say the unthinkable caused my heart to race. What I didn't expect though was for it to come from my mother.

"If things...if things don't work out. Well, there are options, Donald. We don't have to shoulder this burden if we're not ready." She said it as though it had been lingering in the back of her throat for a long time with a death grip on her tongue.

"You haven't thought of...ending the pregnancy have you?" Dad did not ask it because he was disgusted, or because that was what he wanted. He asked it because he had clearly thought the same thing and was shocked to hear his wife relaying the same thoughts.

"It's still early, Donald. We've only been married for just over a year and we're still so young," she drew each word out carefully, inspecting it before pulling the next. "It's an option. Or adoption, I'm sure there are thousands of couples dying to have a child of their own."

"You have thought about this then?"

"Of course I've thought about this. What else am I going to do all day?" Mom finally broke and the tears started to flow, soft sobs breaking apart her words, "You're out looking for work…and I don't know how things will be two weeks from now."

The sound of tears continued as neither of them spoke for a few long minutes. I was still in shock about hearing the words come out of their mouths, *"ending the pregnancy… adoption."* How could they not want me? Everything was planned so carefully and I was destined for this family. What would happen if they rejected me now? Scenes from Jeremiah's childhood repeated in my head as I waited for another word from either of my parents.

I needed for one of them to say something comforting, to do away with the thoughts they had vocalized. I needed something to come between their fear and my fate. If only I was big enough to do or say something.

Nothing happened though and eventually it became all too clear that they had said all that they would say on the matter, leaving it open to discuss later.

"I'll call Jason tomorrow and ask him about the job. I still don't think he can help me, but I'm tired of this constant worrying. If nothing comes up in the next week, we'll talk things over and discuss our options." Dad spoke matter-of-factly, trying to soothe Mom.

The tempo of her heart remained steady throughout most of the conversation but picked up now as she slowed her tears.

"Donald, this shouldn't be so hard. Why did everything have to happen at the same time? It's not fair."

"I know Carrie. It isn't fair. But, we'll figure it out. Yes, it will all work out." In a stark change from only a few weeks before, Dad was now reassuring Mom.

It all sounded good on the surface, but I could tell that his comforting words were inflated, an attempt to appease his own worries as much as Mom's.

That was the last they spoke on the matter that evening.

If I could have cried, surrounded by the comforting but oddly alienating fluid of my mother's womb, I would have.

Chapter 7

12 Weeks

Before the last time Jeremiah left Heaven, we spent a lot of time watching old acquaintances from above. From so far away, their lives looked quaint and peaceful, thumbtacks on a giant map that occasionally moved from one place to another. But, to me they were more; I knew those thumbtacks. They were old friends, friends I had spent years with learning and observing the world below.

Jeremiah always enjoyed looking in on those old friends, gleaning what he could from their experiences in preparation for his own. I took a bit of pride in reprimanding him for it at times. I trusted in the instructions I had received and didn't want to spend all of my remaining years before entering the Earth, contemplating the experiences of a thousand others.

Admittedly, there were a few times when curiosity got the best of me and I ended up spending more time than Jeremiah watching my old associates thrive on Earth. I'm sure somewhere in the details of their lives were lessons for me whether I learned them or not. Details that would have definitely proved beneficial to me now. It's really too bad that I spent so much time watching instead of studying, the difference is often so very subtle.

However, when it came to Jeremiah things were a lot different. He was so intriguing that one would learn from him without even trying. After Mom and Dad's conversation the other day, I found myself returning to some of those memories of and conversations with Jeremiah that seemed meaningless at the time. It wasn't obvious to me then but now I know everything meant something with him. There was no room for nothingness. Every dead awkward silence Jeremiah placed between us had meant something or at least part of something.

The other day, I couldn't help but wonder why he wasn't more like God, simply revealing the answers to all of my questions. I immediately took back my thought, knowing it was impossible for any of us to be exactly like God, free of insecurities and shortcomings.

There was one time in particular when Jeremiah and I were quietly observing the first day of school for Cecile. She was almost five years old at the time, living in the South Paris suburb of Montrouge. We had known her before when she was Cecile, an Angel of Heaven. Nationalities came after birth, one of those labels that doesn't truly exist until you're on Earth.

Cecile had no doubt forgotten who we were years

beforehand. Neither Jeremiah nor I had forgotten her though or the years we spent listening to her recite her earthly instructions. Her tenacity and focus were unrelenting, there was no doubt she would remember her purpose.

Julien had just cracked the door to the humble corner apartment he shared with his family. He was in the process of squeezing out of the door to avoid the inevitable moan of the rusty steel hinges when Cecile pounced on him. The door wailed as it opened the rest of the way under the weight of Julien and Cecile stumbling backwards.

From inside, the faint voice of Adele, Cecile's mother, rang out, "Julien! La porte…"

"Je sais!" He bellowed back before repeating it again to himself, "je sais."

Cecile's hundred watt grin, splitting a wedge in her face from ear to ear cut him short though as he whisked her into his arms. He squeezed her just the right amount and set her back down with a grunt and a smile.

With a ruffle of her hair, he reminded her to be careful for what must have been the millionth time in her short lifespan, "Faites attention, Cecile."

"Oui, Papa."

He kissed her forehead and waved goodbye, "Au revoir. Passe une bonne journee."

The two parted ways and Cecile bounded her way back inside to where Adele was waiting with a clean dress and the nice black shoes she had purchased especially for that day. When her mother held the dress up, Cecile wailed like a child half her age knowing that going to school meant being separated from her mother.

I laughed heartily, wondering how such an excitable little girl would one day become a leader in the Western Hemisphere.

"How soon until she's late for the first day of school?" Jeremiah asked from my right.

"Probably just a few minutes."

"Think she'll make it?"

"Ha ha, it's a tossup."

We watched a little while longer as Adele began chasing her daughter with a flower-print dress in one hand and a black wire brush in the other. "Cecile!"

Unfortunately, that day, Michael and Joshua, two Angels we often shared our daily observations with stole our attention.

"Cecile giving her mother the run around today?" Michael chuckled.

"First day of school. This time it actually counts for something," I said.

"You should leave those two alone for now. Rose's parents just found out." Joshua was eager to relay the news and understandably so. The moment of revelation was almost as celebrated as departure.

Jeremiah shifted his attention almost immediately, "Rose?"

"Yes. It's been eight weeks already." Michael said it nostalgically, as though eight weeks was any measure of time for an Angel.

"What were their names again?"

"Jacqueline and Brian. Newlyweds in Colorado, both school teachers."

"What are we waiting for then?"

The four of us shifted our focus to the small suburb of Chatfield Acres, Colorado where two young school teachers were sitting on the edge of a Queen sized bed with a tiny white stick in hand, its blue smiley face looking up at them.

Jacqueline, Rose's future mother, spoke first, "This is...this is...wow."

"What are we going to do, hun?" Brian's face was firmly planted between his hands.

"I don't know. This is just too soon. We're not ready for this right now. Our careers are just getting started." Jacqueline started crying while Brian tried to find somewhere else to look.

"What are we going to do?" Brian repeated his question, this time more forceful.

"The clinic is open on Monday. I can stop by after class."

"Jackie, are you sure?" Brian asked the question, but he seemed to agree with her assessment.

"We can't do this right now and you know it."

"I know. But, are you sure this is what you want?"

"Why? Do you want to keep it?"

"No. Well, I mean….I don't really know, hun. I didn't think this day would come for a few more years…you know, when we're ready."

"Me neither."

"This is a big decision. It's still Friday. Let's take the weekend to think before we make any final decisions, okay."

Jacqueline wiped the tears from her cheek, "That's a good idea. Let's just take a couple days."

Back in Heaven, the four of us watched intensely, but I could tell my companions were as confused and upset as I was by what was happening below. Michael's brow furrowed into a twisted knot while Joshua looked as though someone had punched him hard in the midsection. Jeremiah's reaction was the most interesting though. The crooked tilt of his mouth and the shadow beneath his eyes betrayed anger. I had never seen Jeremiah angry before, nor many angels for that matter.

"They don't want her?" Michael spoke first.

"No," Jeremiah said, "they don't."

"She didn't leave too early did she?"

"No. She had everything in order. She received her instructions and left at the right time," Jeremiah affirmed.

"I don't understand then," Joshua added.

Silence fell over us for a few more minutes as the two who had never been to Earth before contemplated what they knew must surely be the answer; something horrible would happen to Rose. Jeremiah alone seemed to fully understand the implications, but said nothing.

After what appeared to be a momentary flashback, Jeremiah finally spoke, "She will be back in a few days. You should prepare to comfort her. Returning early is not an easy experience."

That was the last any of us said about Rose. Three days later she returned. For days she would stare in the distance for long periods of time then on rare occasions she'd spend time conversing with Jeremiah. I overheard her tell him that when she prayed for God to change her parent's mind, He reminded her that He offers gentle persuasion but doesn't strong-arm anyone, free will is still paramount.

In time, Rose regained some of the excitability and joy we had known for decades, but she was very much like Jeremiah whenever I brought up the matter of her return, she fell into silence.

Until now, I never understood them ending a conversation whenever I mentioned their fateful return. It didn't make sense until this very moment- they were deeply troubled. The idea that their parents would reject them, one of God's most magnificent gifts, must have been almost unbearable.

I understood finally, because now I was terrified. My parents never said the word I knew meant my immediate return, *abortion*, but I knew what *ending the pregnancy* meant and what the result would be. It meant my body being physically torn apart and my spirit departing from it, returning to an angelic state in Heaven. *Would they really do that to me?*

The morning of Mom's twelfth week started like many days from the previous four weeks, with the sound of Dad trying to hold a conversation with Mom from a distance.

Mom had just reminded him of an interview he had with Jason's firm that afternoon.

"I still don't feel right about asking your brother for help."

"Why? Why is it so hard for you to get help from my family?"

"I just don't feel right doing it."

My body bounced to the rhythm of Mom's bare feet slapping against a wood floor, moving beyond the walls that separated them- I presumed.

"Well, you don't have a choice. It's been almost four weeks now and you still haven't caught a good lead."

The conversation stopped there for a moment as a gentle electric hum – either a tooth brush or razor, I had yet to decide which – replaced Dad's voice.

When the humming stopped, the conversation continued, "Look, I know he's your brother and you two have a close relationship and all that, but he's never liked me and he sure isn't helping me because he suddenly has a change of heart. I just don't like it."

"Well, too bad. Put your suit on."

"Hey, I'm going, am I not?"

"Yeah, you're going," Mom said, "and I really do appreciate it." She paused and took a deep breath. "Look, Jason's a good guy. He doesn't like you because that's how we grew up. He looked out for me and I let him pick on the men in my life. It's every big brother's prerogative. But, I know that he'll do his absolute best to help you get a job though. Don't even think otherwise."

"You don't sound very confident."

"I just don't want you to be upset with him if things don't work out. You two should really get along, you know."

"Yeah," Dad said with a sigh. "Well, here's hoping things

work out for the best."

"And Donald?"

"Yeah?"

"If things don't work out."

"I know. We'll talk about it when I get home tonight."

Mom's familiar morning routine changed that morning. Normally, after Dad left she would see to her own bathroom needs, creating the same ceramic symphony that he did every morning. Next, she would eat. Breakfast was always different, depending on the combination of our cravings. She still won most of the time, but I knew that soon my own growing hunger would begin to affect her decisions.

After breakfast, she would exercise for at least a half hour. The leathery scraping of the rubber mat on the treadmill under her feet was as steady as her cup of orange juice with breakfast or the Thursday afternoon phone calls to her mother.

Nothing went according to routine on this particular day though. No sooner had Dad departed for his interview than I heard the familiar monotone button presses of a phone number.

"Mom? Hi, can we grab some lunch today?..

"I just need to talk to you about some things…

"Okay. I'll see you then."

The call was brief. She didn't have to say much more for me to know what she would be discussing with her mother. Days had passed since the frightening conversation between Mom and Dad regarding my future, but I remembered every single word. With the possibility of Dad's interview not working out, it was time for her to start seriously considering what they had discussed.

It's a miracle that none of the uncertainty on the outside stunted my internal growth. Everything was falling into place within me; my vocal chords were stretching tight, my liver had just begun to start the steady churning of blood that would continue for nearly a century. My ears and eyes had slowly moved into place. The intricate clay-like molding of my body was developing so keenly that it was almost impossible to imagine my Mom preparing to take it away from me.

***

Mom's lunch plans took her into the heart of downtown, a place I had since come to associate with a heightened pulse, stomach irritation and a plethora of undesirable cursing. This is usually how I knew we were in the city. Today however, I was sure that we were outside because of the horns blowing and sudden presence of my grandmother.

"You know there's plenty of parking near the restaurant dear." This was actually the first day I had ever heard Grandma's voice. It was pleasing. She sounded young still, sporting a throaty rasp dabbed with the patience and experience of a woman who knew exactly what everyone else's response would be. It was soothing.

"I know. I just want to get a little exercise. I didn't feel up to it this morning and now I feel guilty."

"Oh, sweetheart. That's normal. With everything that is going on in your body, you should expect some changes."

"It's not that Mom. I just want to stay…stay fit."

"Alright, as you wish."

Right then, we passed near a bitter conversation between two angry sounding men. I normally ignored the sounds of the street, preferring to listen to Mom in the safety of my dim bubble. These two men however, were starting to grow louder and it was hard to ignore their bizarre conversation. It brought me a moment of levity.

"I don't care if there's a whole freaking herd on the road. You be here on time. Where do you live anyway – a zoo?"

"Hey, you know as well as I do that those Lambs Farm jerks…"

"The amusement park? You got held up by the amusement park. What are you, eight?"

"I wasn't petting the stupid goats. I was waiting for them to get out of the road."

"This is rich, Cal. Last week it was a broken sewer pipe,

now a herd of petting zoo goats. Listen. I don't care if a UFO lands on your roof, drags you through a field of manure, and leaves you naked in the middle of a flattened cornfield. Be late for work again and you're fired. Period."

Cal started to argue again, but the voices were growing quieter as Mom and Grandma kept walking, tearing themselves from the story of the man being late for work because of goats.

Mom finally said something, "We're here. Doesn't look that busy either. Do you want to grab a table? I need to use the restroom."

"Sure thing, dear."

A few minutes later, after ordering two soup and salad specials and a ham sandwich, Mom and Grandma were discussing the weather.

I had noticed in my recent months on the inside that adults liked to talk about the weather. It was a universal variable and no one ever disagreed with anyone else. If someone said it was nice and sunny, no one stepped in to argue that it was in fact raining or that the sun was not nice. In terms of easy conversation, the weather was by far the easiest.

"I hope it stays like this. I could use some sunshine these days."

"Not that this has anything to do with the weather, but how's Donald's job search going?" Finally one of them changed the subject.

Mom sighed as she hesitated in answering. Silverware and glasses clinked against the table and her plate as the silence stretched on for seconds that seemed like minutes.

Finally deciding that she may as well be candid, Mom replied, "Not well."

"He's meeting with Jason today, isn't he?"

"Yes, thankfully. But, I just don't know if he can help. Donald was a great broker, but everyone in the city has his name on their desk right now. Jason just doesn't have that much clout."

"I don't know about that, Carrie. He has a little more *clout* than you think. He just doesn't like to flaunt it."

"So why would he flaunt it now for Donald. Those two hate each other."

Grandma's laugh was tame. It displayed her amusement with the statement and trailed into her next sentence. "Sure seems that way doesn't it? Look dear, your brother is a peculiar person. I love him to death, but he's an odd ball at times. Everything was a job to him, even when he was a boy. When you were born, he acted as though he'd landed the promotion of a lifetime, protecting a little sister. I think it's just hard for him to admit that you're all grown up now, both of you."

"That's all fine and good, but the tension between those two hasn't changed. Things aren't going to work out with this interview, I just know it."

"Do you honestly think your brother would do something to harm you or your baby just to spite your husband?"

"Well, no Mom. I don't think either of them would intentionally ruin this. I just don't think they can actually get along long enough for that to matter."

There was another short silence when the voice of the waiter chimed in, "Okay, who had the black bean and the cobb? Alright, and that must make you the minestrone and the garden...oh and the sandwich. Ladies, if I can't help you with anything else at this time, please enjoy your meal."

His voice trailed away as he started to take a different order a short distance away from Mom's table. Mom and Grandma did not speak for a few seconds longer, probably seasoning their food first.

"Mom, I need to ask you something. It's...kind of hard for me to this bring up."

"Sure dear. What is it?" She sounded worried.

"Donald and I have been talking. With my doctor's visits and everything else coming up, we're not quite sure if things are going to....well, work out."

"Now, don't talk like that. Donald will get a job soon. You wait and see. You must have more faith in your husband."

"That's not just it, Mom. I'm sure he'll get a job eventually. If not, I can start looking too. I'm talking more so about the baby."

"What about the baby?"

"I just don't know if we can afford to have one right now."

"Carrie…" Grandma's voice, full of surprise.

"Donald's savings are only going to last another month or two and his insurance will expire in a couple of weeks. We're just not prepared, Mom. I don't know if this is going to work."

"We could always help out, sweetie."

"No you can't, Mom. It's only been just over a year since the wedding. I know how much you and Dad splurged, you're still paying for it."

"Fine. What do you plan on doing then?"

"That's why I asked you to have lunch with me today. I needed someone to talk to about this. Donald and I have discussed it to some small degree and we think it might be best not to have a child right now, if things don't work out with this job interview."

I expected cries of outrage from Grandma, a supporter in my corner decrying the act that Mom and Dad seemed to be getting closer to every day. Yet, her voice remained quiet. For me, every second she remained calm and supportive for her daughter, I grew more and more paranoid. "You're thinking of ending it for real?" she finally asked.

"We brought it up, yes."

"I don't know what you want me to say to you, Carrie. I know what you're going through right now. I was there when Jason came along."

"You were older, Mom. You were ready."

"No one is ever ready, dear. If they were, they would be too old to have children."

Mom forced herself to laugh at her mother's joke, possibly accepting the small bit of advice that it contained.

"This is a monumental decision Carrie, but one I know you and Donald will think through carefully before making. Whatever you decide, I'll be there for you. You know that, right?"

"You're not going to give me any advice, then?"

"You know I think it's wrong. But is that really going to affect your decision?"

"That's what I thought you'd say."

"You and I both know you didn't come here for me to tell you not to do it or to give you my permission to go through with it."

"Really? Why am I here then?" Mom's voice quivered with the effort of withholding tears and remaining civil towards her mother.

"You're here because you're scared."

"Of course I'm scared Mom. Look, I don't think I want to talk about this anymore."

"I understand. But let me at least give you this small piece of advice. Don't make a short-term decision that can produce long-term consequences."

From there the conversation went back to the weather and those petting zoo goats. Mom didn't mention Jason, Dad, or me again. I was beginning to feel like a murderer since mentioning my presence killed a conversation in seconds.

While normally an excursion into the city would have been an interesting experience, a chance to listen to men argue in the street, ask for money, or try to sell various kinds of food to anyone within ear shot, I shut everything out that afternoon. I reflected on the years of hard work and careful planning required in bringing Mom and Dad together in the first place. Years at one point, that seemed to go on forever until everything fell in place and I finally made it here.

Yet, after what seemed like another lifetime – in truth only twelve weeks, but for the metamorphosis I have undergone, it may as well have been a lifetime – some sort of end was rapidly approaching.

WOMB CHILD

***

Dad returned to the house shortly after Mom and I did. Sounds I had grown to both love and fear informed me that he had just thrown closed the front door and was trudging towards us. Floorboards creaked in unison as the silence of two adults unsure of their futures collided.

"How did it go?"

Dad didn't answer at first. After weeks of hearing Mom ask '*how did it go*', I was hoping he had a good news. "Jason was nice."

"Not Jason. How did the interview go?"

"They're looking to go younger, promoting within. They're doing what every other firm in the city is doing, promoting interns at entry level salaries. But I'm supposed to go back tomorrow and interview with another department."

"Well, that sounds encouraging."

"It's just a bunch of…you know, I just don't understand. I was a great broker. I still am. Maybe I shouldn't have yelled at Hartzman on the phone like that."

"Hey, now. You know as well as I do that he had it coming. Don't feel bad for telling that jerk how you felt."

"Yeah, but I *sure* can't find a job now."

"Don't start acting like this is over. You still have an

interview tomorrow. And Jason really couldn't offer you anything in his department? He runs it, doesn't he?"

"Well yeah, but with the way the bureaucracy builds up in these places these days, he doesn't have more than a small say in the hiring process. Human resources takes care of all that."

"That doesn't make any sense."

"Corporate America. Gotta love it."

"At the law firm, HR didn't decide who got a job. If a partner wanted an employee, they hired the employee."

"Half these brokerages don't have more than two or three partners anymore. Anyone important knows everyone else who's important. Unfortunately, Hartzman is important."

"What a mess."

Dad let out a boisterous grunt as if to exhale some unspoken concern. "Tell me about it," He said before shuffling away.

Silent enveloped their discussion while Mom began bustling about with kitchen utensils, their familiar clanging sing-song rang alongside her belly and my ears.

After a few minutes passed, she raised her voice to call her husband back to her. "Donald, I know you've had a rough day, but we need to talk about a few things."

Seconds later, he replied, "Yeah…I know. I was just hoping we could relax for a little while first. Maybe eat dinner."

WOMB CHILD

"No. We've been relaxing and waiting for too long already. We need to figure this out now. It's important."

"Okay. Let me just change out of this suit really quick."

"I'll follow you up."

"Alright."

The reluctance on the part of either of my parents to simply say what they already knew they were going to say was impossible for me to withstand. I had listened for days on end already as they argued with, prodded, questioned and suggested to each other that they needed to talk about "some things", those things being me and my life. The pit of boiling tar that replaced my stomach seemingly days before continued to broil my insides, every one of my nerves on the edge of a gaping cliff, afraid yet now growing impatient.

"It's time to talk about the baby. I can't put this off any longer and I won't let you either."

"Okay. So, what do you want to do?"

"We talked about this last week. If the job with Jason fell through we weren't going to have enough money to last more than another month or two."

"I know that already."

"And your insurance runs out in less than a month."

"Also something I know."

"Don't do this, Donald. I'm just laying out the facts."

89

"I'm sorry…it's just, I really didn't want it to come to this."

"Well it has and we need to deal with it." Mom's voice did not quiver or hiccup as I expected. It was cold and matter-of-fact as everything she said hit its mark. She already had her mind made up. "I'm going to get up early tomorrow and go to the clinic."

"You're sure then?"

"Look, we don't have a choice here. We can't afford to keep living like this and a baby would only make things harder. What about the medical bills? Do you think we can afford those? We both need to look for work right now and we can't do that effectively while I'm pregnant. It just adds to the stress."

"You're right. I know you're right. It doesn't make it any easier to hear, but I know you're right. Sooo…" Dad drew the word out sounding like he was avoiding going any further. "What time are we leaving in the morning?"

"I'm going alone."

"What? No, you're not. Why can't I be with you?" Dad questioned sounding almost indignant.

"Because, I need to do this alone. Besides, you have an interview in the morning."

"You and I both know that interview is a waste of time and I'll be shooed out of the building in less than twenty minutes.

Forget the interview. I'm going with you."

"Donald, this is already hard enough. I couldn't handle it with you there, okay? I have to do this by myself. I just need this to be over so we can move on. I want to get off of this rollercoaster and pretend as if this ride never happened."

"But Carrie..." Dad cut himself short, deciding not to continue.

"No! I said no. You are not skipping an interview either. I don't care if you walk in and they start laughing, you sit through that interview and you impress those fools. Someone out there's bound to be a good person, not stuffed firmly in Hartzman's back pocket."

"Alright. Okay. I'll go. And I'll be here as soon as you get home waiting. If I'm not, call me right away. I want to know exactly how it went."

"Sure. I'll give you a call."

A volcanic surge of emotion erupted within me and a gush of pain, hot and determined, coursed through my head. I couldn't take it any longer and stopped listening to their conversation. It was probably going to turn into the same mindless chatter I'd heard that morning in the restaurant about rain clouds and lazy goats. I just didn't care anymore...but still mourned for the countless number of so many others who had gone through this same situation, felt the same rejection as I was feeling right then.

I do not believe Jeremiah or Rose knew beforehand that their time was limited. That their parents would have unwittingly pronounced their sentence upon them just as mine had done, giving me the final hours to remember everything I had ever been told and everything that had ever been said.

I spent years receiving instructions from God as to my purpose here on Earth. He told me exactly who my parents would be and exactly how they would raise me so that one day I could change the course of human history for the better. I spent years listening to Jeremiah give me instructions on how to bring my parents together and how quickly you forget once you are born. He spoke of humanity as though it were some distant artifact that he studied on occasion, not the world into which we all strived to be born one day.

No one ever told me what I should do if my parents decided they didn't want me. So, I shut them out and remembered everything else everyone had told me, all the good things I was supposed to experience and tried my hardest to forget all of the bad. Like no other time since being on Earth, my spirit from within compelled me to communicate with my Father.

I drew my limbs in closer to my chest, tightening the fetal position and allowed the tepid liquid surrounding me to wash away my fears and relax my mind. The melodious chorus of

WOMB CHILD

Mom's internal organs blended to form a composition like that of a masterful 18th century composer. There could be no better place to rest on Earth.

I finally made my request known. "God, my Father, please help me. Why does it seem you have forsaken me?"

Almost immediately, I heard three words that I did not understand echo within my heart. "It is finished."

Chapter 8

12 Weeks

The voices were clear, wave upon wave of anger voiced in a combination of eerie chants and forceful curses. The sea of sound undulated, its tide breaking against an occasional rock in the crowd. Every direction on which I focused my attention revealed another new voice announcing disapproval.

I had made it my goal while waiting for my time to leave Heaven not to look down on the world in curiosity. Unlike so many of my peers, I chose not to focus on the evils of the world believing that ignoring them could somehow make my future life easier. Since the moment I learned my purpose, I decided I would rather *experience* the world than try to understand it. So, the violent exclamations from dozens of unhappy men and women were now hard to absorb.

Mom had awaken early that morning. I heard Dad's snoring louder than ever before, probably victim to thoughts that had worn him out completely. The reversal of their positions, Mom splashing water and tapping her toothbrush noisily while

Dad slept held a certain amount of irony that I found it hard not to be a little perturbed.

A gentle morning, a familiar glass of orange juice and thirty minutes piloting the gravely belt of a treadmill would normally have warmed my heart, but this morning's routine felt more like the final rights before my walk to the gallows.

Now, after the steel rattle of the engine subsided and Mom closed the car door, the assault of the crowd reached me, shattering the false security of a familiar morning routine. Slowly the chants began to coalesce, taking on meaning as I separated the voices from each other.

"Every life is precious!"

"Murder is not the answer!"

"God is always with you!"

They were cheering for me! I realized it and immediately recognized the effect their words were having on Mom and her forward march. She had been tense all day. I could feel a combination of both mild nausea and a stiff determination that made her muscles tense. She didn't savor what she was about to do and these men and women were upsetting her even further.

I cried out along with them, not caring that only I and other nearby fetuses within their mothers could hear. *I am alive. I deserve a chance. I have a purpose here that will prove beneficial to all mankind. You have no idea of the impact or severity of your decision.* Joining in their chorus of what had originally sounded like anger, I recognized it as something else. It was love and I was a part of that love.

Mom tripped and I tumbled inside of her, the rush of blood to my head disrupting my earnest protest. "No, no thank you. I'm really in hurry." She said it quickly, spitting out the words like a shiny red ball, thrown to distract a small pet.

"It's not too late. You can still do the right thing. You can choose life."

"I...I... I really need to be going now."

"Just give me a minute of your time and I promise you won't be in a hurry any longer."

"Please...just leave me alone." A sob drowned out much of the word *leave* and Mom began to cry.

"The pain this is causing you. Do you see it? You don't want to do this."

Mom did not reply, but continued crying, the voice of the man now behind her.

A new voice, the tiny adolescent voice of a child greeted her now, "Ma'am, you shouldn't go inside. Every life is important. Every life comes at the right time and your baby's time is right now." A soft lump rose in my throat as I recognized the words I had repeated to myself so many times before. Could this girl, whoever she was, have remembered her instructions- to save me and many others? Had I known her in Heaven? What had she done to remember?

But the voice cut off. Then I began to bounce up and down violently. My body twisted and turned in somersaults and cartwheels that I could not control. The currents of water splashing and crashing against my body made it impossible for me to hear anything outside.

Waves of nausea spidered through my veins, only persisted by the constant up and down motion of what must have been Mom running. What was she running from…or toward?

The voices of those kind souls outside had given me yet another degree of hope; but now, her fright had taken hold of me and nothing made sense anymore. The constant motion of fluid sloshing around and through my ears still blocked the sound of those voices and of my Mom. *How could she be in such a hurry to do this to me?* I wailed against what now felt like a prison wall.

Still flipping around within, I felt what little control I had maintained slip away as the terror took hold. I couldn't go back above. It would be generations before another opportunity presented itself and everything would have gone wrong by then.

No one could be my parents except *my parents*. My heart beat faster than I knew it could, drawing taut against the thin layer of skin I had yet to finish growing. Despite my blindness, I shut my eyes tighter and held myself, even as I twisted around inside my mother.

Nothing had happened the way it was supposed to. Everything I had been prepared for, the loving recognition of a baby boy, the months of closeness to my mother inside the womb – none of it meant anything and I was only seconds away from being sent back to Heaven where I would watch as my parents went on with their lives without me and the world went on with its wars. How could this have happened?

But, it was the sudden stop that shocked me more than anything. In the midst of an ominous realization that the world was not as loving and caring as I had once expected and hoped, I stopped moving and heard once more the sounds of the men and women's voices. Only now, they had stopped talking and were cheering. The thunderous applause and whooping cheers of dozens of people were reassuring. What had happened? Where was the girl who remembered?

The cheering died down with the familiar expansion and click of a metal door latch. I was once again alone with Mom. She was sobbing, soft yet uncontrollably. For what seemed like an hour, the car remained still with the sound of nothing but her gentle weeping. I could no longer hear the cries of the crowd outside, but I thanked them anyways, blessing them in their work.

Whoever they were and for whatever reason they had taken up such a cause, their shouts had changed everything. I wanted to comfort my mother, but I knew the tears were not all in sadness; grief and joy can occasionally become one. What I hoped Mom felt was not just the empty and cold revelation of what she had almost done, but the possibility of what the future might hold and what I might hold for her and her husband in the coming years. I hoped somewhere within her guilt and grief there was truly a measure of joy.

Something came over me in that moment. It was a sense of purpose and loyalty to my cause for being there. Whether Mom knew it or not, she had just saved millions of lives. Most importantly, she had saved mine.

Chapter 9

12 Weeks

I had only been on Earth for three months and had yet to see a single inch of it from eye level. I still had six months in my mother's womb – six glorious, living, breathing months – and I had no idea if things would look the same as they did from the aerial view. But, no matter how majestic and beautiful the world truly was, nothing could compare to the moment Mom turned that car on and drove us back to Dad and our home.

For the first time in what seemed like weeks, I finally felt accepted by my parents. It was a subtle revelation at first, if only because I never allowed myself to recognize before that moment that there was a choice in the matter. Everything always seemed so well established. When God handed out assignments, He never mentioned that things may look like they are going off course or what should be done to redirect the course. Maybe because we would mess it all up.

Only minutes away from losing everything I had worked so hard for, I realized that nothing was quite as simple or as straightforward as it originally appeared. Plans were all fine and good, but human beings depended on each other and even the most noble of causes can be forever altered or interrupted by a single errant action.

It gave me a chance to appreciate the work given to me for my trip to Earth. Too many years had passed since I first learned of my destiny and the magnitude of it had long since faded. With the thought of sitting snuggly in the comfort of my home for the next six months though, I felt a renewed sense of wonder at the goal I was destined to accomplish.

In truth, every child is given their destiny before their spirit enters Earth. No one is born before their time and no one is sent without a purpose. Those who return or whose parents reject them often confuse the order of things. It is not their fault of course. Destiny is a fickle beast, the kind that does not take kindly to tampering. When the parents of a child reject their role in that great big tapestry, things tend to go wrong. I had seen as much of it as I could stand when Jeremiah's second set of parents did not last past his third birthday.

He never truly revealed to me what his destiny actually was, but I managed to glean bits and pieces from others. At some point he was supposed to have developed a cure for one of many incurable cancers that plagued so many people on Earth. His was to be one of the premiere advancements in medical science for the span of a century. But, when something went wrong and he returned to Heaven, the medical industry was unknowingly set back for decades. It was as though someone had taken a pair of shears and snipped the thread to which they were connected.

My destiny is a gem, one that I now carry close to my heart, constantly turning it over in my tiny fingers to witness the flawlessness of its natural design. I am one of those few, like Cecilie, who is chosen for an incredible purpose, a noble and just cause and though God never speaks more highly of one person's destiny than another's, I knew that I had been given one of those truly rare gems.

My parents, both of them good, decent people, would raise me to be a thinker and a problem solver. I'd draw inherently from my multi-ethnic heritage, African, Asian, Jewish and Russian. I would attend the best colleges in the world and study with the smartest men and women in each of them. I would spend the better part of my life studying the interactions between societies, enthralled by the intricacies of so many cultures coexisting on one planet.

Eventually, my knowledge and innate passion for the world around me would lead to a position in one of the world's most dangerous regions, among the world's two most volatile countries. It was not every day that God assigned an Angel the role of an International Diplomat. It was rarer still that such a diplomat would become the one individual who could finally bring peace to a region torn by unthinkable violence and derision for thousands of years. Yet, that was my destiny, one that was vital to the well being of mankind.

Therefore, it was not with selfishness alone that I rebelled against the possibility of my mother so easily rejecting me.

Of course, the relief I felt at my salvation was mercilessly brief. I was given the duration of a car ride from the clinic, back to home where Dad was waiting for Mom to return with an empty womb.

My mother finally managed to place the key in the lock on the front door after numerous failed attempts and Dad's voice greeted us at the threshold.

"Hun, you're back so soon. What happened?"

"I couldn't go through with it, Donald. I just couldn't do it."

"Honey... it's okay."

Mom started sobbing again. "What are we going to do? We can't afford a baby right now. And I couldn't even do anything about it..."

"Come here." Mom's crying, now muffled.

My position was one of conflicting emotions. I wanted more than anything to feel safe and at ease with my parents, but I hated to hear them so upset and worried because of me.

"We're going to get through this, Carrie. Have I ever let

you down?"

"But, the baby, Donald…what do we do about the baby?"

"We still have another option."

No! I immediately remembered the other option they had mentioned the week before – adoption. They couldn't possibly be considering that now, after everything that had just happened. Mom wanted to keep me. She couldn't let this happen.

"Adoption?"

"You don't have to worry about the clinic and we'll know that someone with the proper means will take care of the baby," Dad offered.

You have the proper means, I bellowed from within. *I am your baby.* Why couldn't they hear me? Why wasn't I a part of this conversation?

"I suppose it is an option." Mom took an extensive breath through her nose, pulling deep and hard prolonging the sniffle. She sniffed again two or three times then spoke more clearly, "True, someone would care for it."

*Him. Him. I'm a Him- not an it. Do you believe referring to me as **it** will make this easier for you?*

"What choice do we really have left?" Dad questioned.

Keep me.

"You are right. We can't bring a child into the world right now and keep it. Our lives are a mess."

You can. I'm already here!

"Exactly," Dad agreed. Where do we start though?"

"We can do the research and start making calls tomorrow."

They kept discussing the matter, unknowingly ignoring me and my cries from the inside. I felt as though nothing had changed. Now, instead of returning above, I would be raised by the wrong parents. How could I attend the right schools and learn the right values if I was going to be subject to the care of two strangers, a man and a woman I had never seen before?

This was almost as big of a problem as the morning's trip to the clinic and after only an hour or so of relaxation, my heart's hummingbird pace had returned. What was I going to do now?

Chapter 10

20 Weeks

"Hurry up. We only have an hour before we're supposed to be there." Mom announced.

"Do we really have to go through this so early? You still have four months left." Dad's voice, groggy.

"I don't know, hun. I just know that if we want that assistance, we need to be at the office by nine."

"Okay, I'm moving. I suppose you're already ready to go then?"

"Of course I am. I've been awake since five."

"Someone is nervous."

"No, someone can't sleep lately because someone else has gotten in the habit of kicking my kidneys every morning about two hours before I plan on waking up."

That early morning kick would be courtesy of me and the goal is not to hurt my mother, but to draw further attention to myself. I never thought I would become one of those children who eagerly seeks out attention by acting out, especially not before I was born. I remembered Cecile's early morning tackles with her father and impromptu hide and seek games with her mother, always hoping to draw yet another bit of attention to herself by sending her parents into fits.

Cecile's attitude didn't last long, as is the case with most young children. She eventually grew up a bit and became a proper young French girl. I grew to miss that rambunctious tyke, though.

During the first days of school, Cecile started learning the basics of the French alphabet, knowledge she so proudly shared with her father every day. She would walk in tiny little circles in front of Julien as he peeled his loafers off following a long day of work.

"Ahh….Beh…Ceh…Deh…Eff.."

"No, no. Ahh, Beh, Ceh, Deh, *Uuh*," he would calmly remind her.

"Oui papa. Je comprends."

"Bon. Essai encore."

The two would remain in their positions – Cecile reciting her letters and Julien listening – for over an hour until Adele reminded them of it being time for dinner.

Cecile took to school with a fervor only a few can maintain. Yet, she managed to keep hers for much of the years that followed, her father studiously listening every night as she recited the names of French and German presidents, the roots of Latin words, or the first and second laws of physics.

Cecile's English and German became as impeccable as her French. This accomplishment was largely due to her spending nearly as much time at the Library as she did in the increasingly tiny dining room in which her father quizzed her.

Around Cecile's 9th birthday, a second child was born into the family, Marc Anthony, who was an immediate a hit in the suburb of Montrouge.

Cecile had been nearly three years old when her family moved into the close knit neighborhood and had almost immediately instilled in the neighbors the image of an insufferable child. However, with Marc the neighbors were fortunate enough to know him from birth, from those first perfect months when a child can do no wrong and cannot possibly be any more adorable.

On Marc's fourth birthday, a sunny day in early September, I recall watching Cecile stalk across the bare wooden floors in her floral-decorated bedroom, a room she often spent time in reading when not in the library.

Her library days had dwindled in those recent months as the call of puberty reached her. A call she often took in private while undergoing her inevitable teenage metamorphosis.

"Cecile, s'il vous plait." Adele was calling for her daughter to come down stairs. Everyone, including a few neighborhood boys, was ready to eat the birthday cake and get on with Marc's celebration.

"In one minute," Cecile replied. She had developed a habit of speaking in English as much as possible, probably a response to her lifelong dream of spending a summer in America.

"Cecile! En Francaise!" Adele demanded, wanting her daughter to speak the mother language at all times as if speaking in English would some how diminish or pollute her French heritage.

"Oui." She said weakly descending the stairs to greet her brother.

"Cecile!" A little mop-haired Marc bounded towards his sister, pulling at her dress.

"Marc, arretez!" Cecile nudged Marc away from her slightly, smoothing out her dress in the process.

"Mama! Papa! Cecile est ici!" He continued smiling and ran away from her, into the kitchen where their parents were talking with the parents of the boys attending the party.

"Ah, Bon." Adele returned to the room, pulling Julien behind her. His mouth was wrapped around a slice of bread, a remnant of dinner.

Watching this scene, as Marc deliberately climbed upon the highest chair sitting beside the table and leaned over the cake to blow out the candles…as Adele and Julien smiled and hugged each other with the familial love that only a truly committed family can display, I knew that Cecile would be alright.

Although, her teenage moods were sometimes volatile and her attitude towards her family- indifferent, at the best, there was an unconditional love that penetrated through all of it. Sure, her parents would chide her for speaking English and chastise her when she did not kiss her brother good-bye in the morning, but all of it was done in love. Cecile knew this and so did I.

Before turning my attention elsewhere on that particular evening, I watched as Cecile eventually picked up her brother into the air and hugged him, smiling reluctantly as her parents joined in the embrace. What a perfect image, I remember thinking – that's exactly what I hope to experience one day.

Cecile's life was as normal as could be expected for a future French President. That's right. That petulant, ordinary and obnoxious teenager would eventually attend Oxford and Princeton and return to Paris as an educated, head strong woman with a desire to affect some degree of change. No one would have known it then, watching her. But Cecile's life was eventually enveloped in a bubble of serenity, exactly as God had planned, and whether she knew it or not, she was at peace for that very reason.

I wanted so earnestly to feel the peace Cecile had experienced. And so, desperate times called for somewhat desperate measures. These days, Mom and Dad had almost completely forgotten that I existed. I suppose that might be a bit of a stretch. They couldn't forget I existed, not with the bi-monthly doctor's visits and the adoption center appointments yet they never said much about me. The best thing I could do in retaliation was to kick with all of my might and hope I landed a pot shot on a stray kidney or intestine. Occasionally, it worked.

However, more often than not, my diminutive stature worked against me. I was still a month or so away from being able to land the sort of punches and kicks I needed to draw attention throughout the day.

I only hoped that when I was born I wouldn't carry this sort of temperament with me. Would you ever think that an International Diplomat started out as a baby who resorted to kicking his mother whenever disgruntled?

So, it was with a combination of shame and calculated mistrust of my parents' intentions that I woke Mom up every morning and hoped for a conversation to begin involving the wayward jerk of my limbs. And it did. So, today was already a good day.

"Isn't it a bit early for kicking? You're only just starting to show."

"I don't make the rules, hun. I just rub the sore spot in my side."

Dad chuckled for a split second before thinking better of

it. "Well, we better get going."

"Yeah, yeah. I'm moving."

Mom and Dad stepped sluggishly, likely because of the early hour, neither of them in a hurry to leave for the appointment they had been discussing ever since they received *the call*.

It was two days ago exactly when the phone call came at an early hour. I had failed that particular day to land a blow directly enough to wake up Mom and grapple her attention from the soothing dreams that had apparently taken over since they decided my eventual fate.

Nevertheless, the phone did my job for me and jolted them both awake. Dad had answered it and excitedly relayed the happy – and for me, depressing – news that their background check passed the initial phase. They had been scheduled for an interview with Greg and Marie, owners and operators of the agency. They were a step closer to finding a home for me.

The routine I had of thinking about my future and the purpose given to me was falling apart. Memories of my years in Heaven only made the situation more poignant when considering the likely end result of so much hard work and so many carefully maneuvered encounters.

As much as I wanted to hold on to the divine knowledge I had been given, it wasn't working. Everything from God's "It Is Finished" reply to my parents to my purpose was now one big question mark. And to top it all off, I was going to spend the next few hours listening to my parents discuss who would be raising me. The thought of two strangers taking me to school or teaching me to play catch only served as a reminder of Jeremiah and the debacle of his second set of parents.

It wasn't uncommon for me to spend days at a time looking down on Jeremiah, wondering what had gone wrong. The amount of time and energy he had put into his future life had been inspiring and I had taken most of what I knew from him. How was it that so much had fallen apart so quickly? Could it be that his parents never remembered that part of their assignment was to raise and guide their child to achieve his greatest potential? Did my parents also have this spiritual amnesia in regards to raising me?

It was almost as if Jeremiah's destiny was striking back, like an irritated rattlesnake coming at you without warning. And there would be a million or so people unknowingly affected by this. As unfair as it may seem when his first parents rejected him, they also rejected the answer to many people's health problems.

But no matter the point at which one is rejected during his life cycle, the results are often very costly. Jeremiah would prove this true, time and time again. At first, he was merely withdrawn from his caregivers then months later, he began isolating himself at school.

Everyone thought Jeremiah was going through an adjustment period and that his behavior was just a mere stop on the path to eventual success. I personally saw my old friend make that stop, but never witnessed him finding the other path.

The day Jeremiah turned thirteen, he was traipsing down the dusty road from his grandparents' colonial-style manufactured home in the outskirts of Savannah, the deep shadows underneath his eyes, small furry patch of extra hair between his eyebrows and crooked toothed smirk belonged to an unpleasant child who could possibly become an unpleasant man. He had forgotten his purpose and it showed all over his face.

Although, Jeremiah did not have any good friends, he did end up making acquaintances with a few street kids who introduced him to the "art of getting high". It was then I realized how glad I was that no one else was still following Jeremiah's life. The rest of his friends and Heavenly acquaintances redirected their attention elsewhere as soon as his parents broke up, upset by the failure it represented- an unnecessary distraction.

I supposed that he would one day become the man he was destined to be but the painstaking process was too much for me to bear, day in and day out. After a few years, I also stopped watching Jeremiah yet often wondered if the winds of life would some how blow him to his purpose.

My months in the womb hearing the constant phone calls

and early morning discussions of downtown meetings reminded me of how my parent's choice may alter the course of my life as well.

But what would it really mean for me? Was I going to turn to drugs before I became an adult, forget my purpose in life and drift aimlessly in to and out of rehab before settling down uncomfortably in the back alleys of some slum. *I think Not!*

I wish I could tell Mom and Dad that I am a significant living gift designed especially for them.

God, please tell them for me.

***

An hour or so after a rather smooth car ride with my parents conversing genially about the basic non-committal topics – gas prices, mowing the lawn, and the next episode of some police drama – we arrived at our destination. Soon they were being introduced to a man and a woman in the midst of an overtly noisy space.

From every direction the rambunctious whoops and hollers of a building full of children overwhelmed me. I couldn't make out any of what they were saying. The screams and laughter were interchangeable, making it nearly impossible to know who was upset and who was merely trying to play a rousing game of tag.

I found it hard to withstand the constant barrage and focus on my parents and the couple they had just met. Nevertheless, I had to hear the voices of those selected to handle my future, so I shut out the extraneous noise as much as I could.

"Hello. My name is Donald and this is my wife, Carrie."

"Ah yes, the Hillmans. Please, do come in and sit down. This is my wife, Doctor Marie Weaver. I believe we met on the phone and from the big sign outside you can see I'm Doctor Gregory Weaver. You can call me Greg though."

"Thank you. We're not too late I hope."

"No, you're right on time. We just finished getting the last couple of children out of the dining hall."

"Breakfast time in the orphanage, huh?" Dad commented.

The strange man sighed heavily, "Don't get me started. Moving one child from place to place is hard enough. Attach thirty brothers and sisters and see how well things work out."

"I can't even imagine." Mom added.

"No, I can barely imagine and this is life nearly every day. Anyway, enough about the children. Give them a chance and they'll be climbing all over you. We're here to talk about your situation."

"Yes, that we are." Mom's voice, jovial.

"Mr. and Mrs. Hillman. We both know how hard it can be to come to this kind of decision. That is why we request these meetings every couple of weeks – to make sure you are prepared. Think of it as a preparation course."

"What exactly do these meetings entail?" Dad questioned.

"Well, because you've requested financial assistance, we must be absolutely sure you are following through on all necessary doctor's visitations and recommendations. No offense, but there is a certain investment on our part in the well-being of your child. We like to ensure, for everyone's sake, that everything is being properly handled."

His wife spoke up. "What my husband is trying to say, in his typically crude manner, is that we want to be sure you stay healthy. Yours is a stressful situation and we've witnessed in the past what that can do to perfectly healthy women."

"I understand," Mom said. "These past four months *have been* stressful, but we've managed to cope. Your help will certainly be a blessing."

Blessing? She had no right to use that word in this situation. It made me uneasy and despite the frank kindness in the voices of both Doctor Weavers, I did not like them or their philosophy. I suppose I was biased from the start, but the justification of that bias was written plain as day in the actions of my parents.

"It's what we live for, dear. This place…," Greg paused

then continued, "is a chance for troubled situations to find a happy ending. When it's all said and done, that's what we hope to have accomplished."

"I'm going to go make sure the children aren't tying the staff to a flag pole outside. Would any of you like something to drink?" Marie asked seemingly as an afterthought.

"No, thank you." Mom and Dad answered her in unison.

"Just have Greg give me a shout if you change your mind."

A few seconds later, after the gentle sound of a door closing in the distance Greg began to speak, this time in a much more serious voice. "Mr. and Mrs. Hillman, this is a situation that we unfortunately do not see often enough. We rarely deal with infants and when we do it is usually in light of a tragedy. Not very often are both the mother and father present for the adoption process – this makes our jobs much easier. However, my wife and I do understand that it makes your decision much harder. For that, I want to commend you on your decision.

There are hundreds of adoption agencies in Chicago. Choosing us means you are committed to finding the absolute best home for your child." It sounded more like a sales pitch than the empathetic introduction he was trying to relay, but then again my cynicism toward Greg and Marie Weaver had set in the moment I heard their voices. Nothing he said would sound sincere to me now.

"Thank you, Dr. Weaver. Call me Carrie by the way. We'll be seeing a lot of each other, no need to be stuck on formalities."

"Yes and call me Donald. This is not a decision we came to easily and all of the research pointed to you as an ideal service to help us screen for parents. I won't deny that the medical assistance played a small role in our decision as well."

"I understand. Well, Marie should be back in a short while, so why don't we begin with a little bit of paperwork. Always best to get this out of the way first." The grainy sound of a sheaf of papers sliding across a wooden surface was followed by quick, pointed instructions. "The top two forms are confidentiality agreements. All four of us will sign these forms, basically stating that we do not reveal your identities and you do not reveal yourselves to the parents chosen for your child. A more formal agreement will be made after the legal adoption."

Pens scratched noisily across flat surfaces, inking away their right to even see me in the future. "This next form is your agreement to attend these meetings for three months, in alternating weeks. And these last forms are similar to the forms you completed in advance. We just need to verify your personal information for accurate record keeping."

The rapid tempo of pens began once more as Mom and

Dad went to work filling out the rest of Greg's paperwork. Minutes passed before I heard the whisper of the far off door cracking open. "Oh, paperwork already?" Maria questioned, her heels clicking across the floor to us. "Greg, leave the poor folks alone for a little while- why don't you?"

"Better now than later on, right? Get it out of the way first."

"You make a good point. How are you folks doing though? Thirsty or hungry at all."

"No, we're quite alright," Mom replied warmly. The scratching stopped a moment later and their conversation picked back up.

"Alright then, that takes care of the fun part," Greg laughed at his own less than satisfactory joke and continued, "so, what we'd like to do over the course of the next three months is get to know you and your family a little bit better." He raised his voice some as if answering a question that no one had yet asked, "We know that you have already supplied us with detailed family histories, both medical and cultural. However, we find that the interview process is much more effective in getting to know you personally and assisting in choosing of the right parents for your child."

"So, will we be actively participating in the selection then? I thought there was anonymity."

"Oh there is. Your participation is blind. When the time comes, you will screen applicants without the benefit of knowing their names or locations. Think of it as the same manner in which some college professors graded your papers. You only look at the content. We worry about the rest."

"That is a clever way of keeping it all fair, I suppose." Mom sounded as though she were reassuring herself.

For me, it was becoming harder and harder to read her moods. At a time when she and I should be growing closer, I felt more separated from her than ever, unable to discern exactly what she was thinking at any given time. The tidal effect of her emotions on my own was almost impossible to manage anymore. My heart tended to remain in a constant, tailspin, grasping for anything familiar to keep me upright.

"It's the best we can do. We must keep the identity of our clients' safe, but we also want to ensure that your input is included in the decisions at all junctures."

"I... I think I understand," Mom replied hesitantly.

"Good. Well, let's get started then."

There was a series of jarring reverberations as large objects hit the space directly in front of Mom's belly. The fluid around me vibrated in response, shaking me into a slightly sideways position.

"These are a couple of books that we like to offer to

parents who make the decision to remain involved. You do not need to read these for any of our conversations, but they offer a very good perspective on the life you're giving your child and the effect it will have on him or her as they grow older. Don't let the size fool you. I consider them relatively light reading. Marie can tell you I'm not that smart; wouldn't even know where to start on many things if she didn't put my glasses on for me every morning and point me in the right direction."

"And after all of my hard work, sometimes, he still gets things wrong. Poor man." Marie teased.

Against my better judgment, I was starting to like Marie a little bit. Her one-liners and jabs at her husband were mildly humorous.

"Do you see how she hurts me?" joked Greg.

"You asked for it." Marie giggled.

Mom and Dad both laughed politely at the antics of the Weavers, thought forwent the act of actually saying anything.

"Anyways, these are also good books for helping to deal with the separation and loss you're about to experience. I would recommend them more enthusiastically but don't want you to assume I'm more biased to these than some of the others in the stack."

"Yes. All joking aside, we have received positive feedback from parents we've worked with in the past who not only utilized but greatly appreciated the impact these books had on their transition." Marie had taken on the same robotic tone as her husband now and I mused that my like for her might have been a touch premature.

"The first thing we want to talk about though, and probably the only thing we'll discuss today, is your baby. I've read the statement on your paperwork and this is probably the last topic you want to revisit, but I want you to give us more information about why you've decided adoption is the right step for you and your child."

Mom released a heavy sigh as what felt like a cold knife descended quickly through my stomach. It disappeared almost as fast as it had arrived, but it revealed the extent of her discomfort.

Silence continued for only a moment longer before Mom breathed in deeply and began to recount the entirety of the last twelve weeks for the Doctors. She did not leave out any details and I could only imagine what look must have painted Dad's face as she described his failed attempts to get a new job, his absence at the clinic and the days of coldness that passed between them in the interim.

Listening to her recount everything we had been through already, I couldn't help but wonder how it would be possible to ever forget so much after birth. Too many things had happened already and the realization that in almost four months I would be born and possibly forget every detail of these situations and conversations was just so hard to believe.

"So, as you can see, destiny has led us here. Looking down the numerous paths we've had before us, this was the only one that did not seem to lead to a dead end." Mom concluded.

"I appreciate you sharing with us. It's hard to admit the real reasons for a decision like this at times. We are not in the business of taking your child at all costs. We want happiness for as many people as possible, especially the birth parents. If there are no questions, we can end here today."

As they wrapped up their session, I couldn't help but feel disgusted about having to sit, I mean *float*, through six more of them.

After their meeting, my parents indulged in a rare outing, something they had not done since Dad lost his job. Dad's suggested they see a movie while in the city was at first turned down by Mom who worried about the cost of doing so.

A short bout of begging, some carefully worded sweet talk and a missed turn en route to the freeway eventually led them downtown into the midst of a noisy crowd of teenagers cursing at each other.

The movie, an explosive laden affair, the kind that Dad and Grandpa would watch in tandem while their wives talked on the phone, was the only film playing that both Mom and Dad were willing to see. So, the next two hours were spent in the company of Samuel L. Jackson and Colin Farrell, two members of a Los Angeles S.W.A.T. team, trying to stop a notorious druglord with the only thing they had left – stockpiles of firearms.

I wondered what these action films might look like, if they were something I would even be allowed to watch in the coming decades. From the sickly cries and wicked bone crunching sounds bombarding me, I guessed probably not.

Eventually, after hours of noisy punches and messy sounding gun battles, and an hour of small talk – once again ignoring the most obvious topic of conversation available to them, me – Mom and Dad returned home- to *our* home.

With so much time on my hands and so little I could do to affect the world around me, the cold reality of my situation was now polite enough to slip away and allow me to relax in the blankets of familiarity and belonging. For now, this was my family and this was my home.

Chapter 11

28 Weeks

The months of constant disruption and weeks of arguments with the inside of an unhearing womb had sloughed away like dead skin. I continued to hold on to an invisible piece of hope although everything was starting to look hopeless.

This morning started the same as most other mornings in the Hillman household. My parents woke up early as Dad had yet another job interview. In recent weeks he had been forced to take a small loan from his parents – a couple who apparently did not enjoy lending funds to their at 'one time incredibly successful' oldest child. With the weight of money owed to his parents, Dad decided he would immediately start looking into jobs other than those for which he had experience.

So, Dad reworked his resume and started making the rounds with law firms, insurance agencies, and the occasional high school or community college. He was under or over-qualified for each and every job, but had to keep looking or stay home and face a wife who was emotionally drained because of the finances and physically drained from lack of sleep. The latter, of course, caused by yours truly.

That's right – I have yet to discover the secret of how to tell my parents what they are doing wrong. So, I am left with no choice but to resort to the only tools I have, my left and right feet and hands. It doesn't work every day, but the larger I get – and I'm getting quite large, over a foot tall now! – the less she can ignore me.

Doctor Sprigg has long since convinced Mom that the lower back aches and stomach discomfort are typical problems, an opinion I found to be rather inept. I think she would feel downright peachy if I weren't kicking all the time. It makes me wonder if others often kick from within, trying to relay messages to their mothers. If only we had been given some other means of communication.

Mom wasn't without stress during her pregnancy, but at least she was healthy. The litany of tests Dr. Sprigg ran last week – glucose levels, iron content, and something called an Rh test – all came back with favorable results. Proud of the good health Mom was in, I listened as Dr. Sprigg relayed the good news.

"You, my dear, are one of the healthiest women I've ever seen at twenty-eight weeks. Quite impressive. If we could get those kidneys to stop aching, we could slap you on a poster."

"Oh, now please don't go that far, Doctor. I'm just happy

to hear everything is in good order."

"Hmm, yes. I would say that everything is in good order. We'll see you again then next week, yes?"

"Ah…yes," Mom said plainly. "I'll double check with Susan on the way out."

"Very good. Well, keep doing what you're doing," said Doctor Sprigg."

I boomed with pride about our good health. It's too bad that my portion of it was solely for the benefit of someone else. No matter how hard I tried to forget about that, the thought kept racing through my mind, around and around again like a car on a perpetual racetrack.

Not that Mom and Dad's monthly schedule was of much help. Every other Thursday we visited *the Weaver Center for Foster Children and Adoption* in Chicago. Dad's haughty imitation of a newscaster whenever he said that name always made Mom laugh.

The last visit to see the Weavers was only a few days ago. Their conversation didn't interest me one bit- at first, so I tried to ignore them, hoping not to feel any of the hurt that I had come to associate with their voices. Yet regardless of how hard I tried, it was still difficult to completely ignore two people asking my parents personal questions.

As the visits continued, the Weavers began to reveal

intimate information about themselves, to help Mom and Dad feel more at ease, I suppose. It turns out that Greg was actually 20 years older than his wife. Marie was much closer to the age of my parents.

It was becoming quite difficult for me to imagine them in the same manner in which I once had. Greg's gravely voice took on greater meaning after learning he was in his 50s and his wife's spry, energetic tone portrayed her youthful exuberance. They are a good team though, each asking the questions that the other didn't think to ask.

Marie spoke softly and was always kind. In my mind she couldn't be more than thirty-five years old, probably wearing a long burlap style skirt and an angora sweater, trying to appear just a touch older to fit in with her husband's world without giving away her age.

I found that I often spent a great deal of time now constructing miniatures and panoramas in my mind from the details I had gathered. Seven months of listening and trying to gauge distance, size, and age created an internal projector. I had no means of knowing how accurate my images were or why now, after so many weeks my mind had taken up the role of film reel, but I enjoyed it all the same.

When considering the Doctors and the lives they had chosen or had chosen them, I thought of what I could be doing in thirty years time (year 2038)- mostly analyzing the dynamics of people and their motivation, and gathering the minute details in conversations that would one day help to save the world.

Then, I'd remember the reason that would probably never happen- because those two Doctors were helping my parents mess up everything by handing me over to folks who are not supposed to be in my life, so they will probably do nothing more than distract me from my purpose.

***

Dad finally returned home a few hours after leaving and relayed that absolutely nothing spectacular had occurred during his job interview. In fact, the entry-level position for which he had applied for had drawn upwards of a dozen different candidates, most of them no more than a year or two out of college.

"Kids. They're all kids. I can't believe I've sunken this low."

"Forget it, Donald. You'll be those kids' boss someday."

"I could be those kids' boss right now if they would give me a chance."

"Just give yourself some time. You're a great worker and we both know it."

"Patience, always with the patience," he laughed as

though the word had taken on some new meaning. "My mother has been leaving messages on my phone."

"The money?"

"Not as straightforward as all that, but yes, the money. She mentioned a slew of different things in a message today. Let's see, I believe we need to watch out for overpriced broccoli, can probably wait a little longer on the tune-up for the car and don't need to bring anything to dinner when we visit next week."

"Since when are we visiting your mother?"

"Since about twelve-fifteen this afternoon when she left me a message saying so."

"Well that should be fun. At least we don't have to bring anything."

"That's not really what she meant when she said it."

"Right, of course not. Cheap wine then?"

"Sounds good to me." Dad agreed.

"So, what do you want to do tonight?"

"I was thinking a little bit of absolutely nothing would suit us both just fine."

"Really now? Because I was thinking we oughta visit the nursery and pick up a couple of new shrubs for the front lawn."

"You're kidding right?" Dad asked sounding surprised.

Mom hissed a wisp of air before breaking out in a certain kind of wicked laughter. "I almost had you, didn't I?"

"What did I do to deserve you?"

"Not sure. Let me know if you figure it out."

After a quiet dinner, the rest of the afternoon was spent huddled on the living room sofa where Dad had suggested they retire to watch a movie that had been sitting in the DVD player for the last three months.

The movie, a gloriously quiet narrative, told the story of three brothers who had left the confines of the country in search of fame and fortune in the city. The brothers eventually met and fell in love with the same girl and start fighting bitterly for her hand in marriage. I believe it was the first time I had ever listened to the narrative of a film with my parents and not been appalled, utterly confused or bored. I wondered if I would ever have brothers.

Soon the movie ended and dinner was in the process of being digested. The assembly line of my mother's digestive system churned away in epic fashion as I savored my own share of the nutrients in Chicken Kiev. When the phone rang, neither of them heard it right away. It shook me to attention though and I waited eagerly to hear who it was.

One by one the springs beneath the couch cushions moaned gently as they were freed from Dad's weight. The phone stopped ringing and only seconds later, the whoop and holler of a man who had just received the one thing in life he wanted more

132

than anything else caused Mom to jump. I no longer jostled around as much when she moved suddenly because I had grown so much. However, the confines of her womb had slowly forfeited its walls to me and I pressed against them hard as she jerked.

"What is it?"

Dad's voice became clear as he reentered the room, "I got it!"

"You got it?" Mom asked. "You mean the job?! You got the job!"

"I got the job."

He got the job! Every miniscule problem and unspoken sacrifice that Mom and Dad had made in the last four months finally exploded in front of them as they realized that their financial worries were finally over.

"The insurance job, right?"

"No. Something much less expected."

"What then?"

"Someone's older brother came through."

"I told you Jason would get you a job!"

"Yes, I will now officially admit that your brother is not all bad."

"Are you kidding me? He's incredible. Just saved our bacon. What did you get hired for?"

"The same position I interviewed for, entry level Project Manager. They're going to bump me up in a few months though, assuming I complete some much needed certifications."

"You're already getting a promotion?!"

"Haha, yeah. I guess I am."

"Well, this makes things easier doesn't it?" Dad said.

"Yeah. Now we can tell your Mom not to worry about Broccoli and tune-ups. And that we can pay her back much sooner than expected."

"Now there's a conversation I've been dying to have."

"You should call her tonight."

"No, tonight we do nothing, remember?"

"Ah yeah, that's right. Tomorrow though, we celebrate," Mom said, "as much as I'm capable, I guess."

"Oh, we'll think of something."

I waited for them to mention the baby, to mention me. The money meant that I could stay with them. They talked about Dad's mom and the bills they hadn't paid. They pined for the wonderful date they would have on the day Dad's first paycheck arrived. And they repeatedly mentioned all of the necessary improvements around the house – including a couple of shrubs. But, once again they didn't mention me.

Chapter 12

35 Weeks

Everything changes when the final weeks of pregnancy arrive. I had been told before that my body would undergo incredible changes in the course of nine months, but nothing prepared me for what happened in the last six weeks or so.

First, the sensations I started feeling were more intense than ever before. Of course, I have always felt things, but this was different. Alongside the emotional rollercoaster I copiloted with my Mom everyday, I felt the extremities of my body spring to life. The freedom of movement, the muscular response – it was all there. I suppose this meant I could feel real pain as well, not the imagined or exaggerated sensations I had been feeling already. This both excited and scared me in equal measures.

I haven't finished growing completely, but it feels as though I could not possibly expand an inch further. Every day, Mom complains that she has turned into a blimp, a massive creature unrecognizable in comparison to her former self. Dad reassures her and is very careful with what he says.

135

At night, Mom rubs her stomach and hums, an action I have come to adore and attribute to the love and recognition I once thought they would never show me. Often, I lose track of her voice as I doze. Other times, I absorb as much as I can, listening with my heart rather than my ears.

It has been more than three weeks since the last visit to the *Weaver Center for Foster Children and Adoption* and I have not heard a single word spoken regarding new parents or paperwork. It was though everything had been decided already and mentioning their plans would somehow ruin them. I knew it would be too much to hope that my parents had simply forgotten about the adoption agency, that they, by default, decided to keep me since the employment situation was resolved.

Dad's new work schedule did not seem to have any affect on my mother's normal routine. In fact nothing seemed to have changed around the house except for Dad being slightly more jovial than before and Mom not airing her worries to Grandma on the phone two or three times a week. So, this morning, when the white noise of Dad's alarm clock buzzed one hour earlier normal, I wondered why.

"This is the last one, right?" Mom said, voice groggy. It was muffled by her mouth being pressed up against what was likely a wad of bed linens.

Dad's voice responded with an equally exhausted tone,

though a bit more pronounced, "Yeah. This is it until the baby's born."

"Thank God. I'm tired of these early meetings."

"No kidding. Do they ever sleep?"

They had not forgotten. They had been waiting. It's impossible to describe the intertwined emotions of fear and resolution that overtook me whenever I thought about my fate. If I have discovered anything in the months I've spent floating here, it's that my reign of influence over them has ended. Yet, for so long my influence was quite substantial. I had maneuvered my parents like pieces on a chess board to meet each other. It was unthinkable to be stuck here listening to their discussions and decisions without having any means to affect them.

Nevertheless, that was the situation I found myself in and whenever I thought I had come to terms with it, an icy tingle coursed from the tip of my largest toe – fully formed now – to the base of my skull. I would shiver, feeling terrified. Images would flash through my mind of Jeremiah wearing a plastic bag over his body during a rain storm, trying to find an awning under which to light a joint and drink his beer in peace. Why couldn't I remember Cecile instead? She had been happy. Her parents spoke to her in the sweet, unfettered French of mature Parisian parents who loved their daughter.

And yet, whenever I closed my eyes now, it was not the

mischievous grin of a five year old bounding away from her mother; it was the sallow, yellow-eyed visage of a man who, as an angel, had been my best friend.

I don't know that I've ever experienced despair before. Surely, I hadn't when I was in Heaven, and until now, hope was always there, however tiny the sliver. But, as I listened in Gregory Weaver's office to him and his wife read through the profile of a couple they believed would make "ideal parents" for me, I felt a weight that must have been much heavier than my heart, fall down the cavern of my throat and settle unevenly in my gut.

"The father is thirty-five years old, an ad-executive for a major electronics company. The mother is thirty-three and currently sits on the school board. She does plan on resigning after the birth of the baby. Both mother and father have been thoroughly screened for any history of criminal activity, drug or alcohol abuse, or family dysfunction. They own a two story Victorian home, paid it off two years ago this October...."

The list went on as Greg regurgitated an entire lifetime's worth of information about this couple. For the first time since I had arrived on Earth, I tried my hardest not to remember. I did not want to remember after I was born that my future "father" was a Canadian through his mother's side or that my future "mother" was a black belt in Judo and had once tried out for the

138

U.S. Olympic Team.

I did not care that either of them sounded like the ideal parents for just about any child or that I now had no idea what my surname would be. If I had gained a tad more dexterity, I would have used my index fingers to plug my ears and ignored everything he was saying.

"They have *not* been told yet that your child will be the one they adopt. They only know that their names have been associated with a child set to be born in a month's time. It is ultimately up to you whether we tell them. Your anonymity remains intact either way."

Dad started to speak, "I don't know that it..."

But Mom cut him off quickly, "Don't tell them yet."

"Alright, we'll keep it quiet for now. It's more of a surprise that way. One last thing before you head out though. This envelope contains instructions for the proceedings. You will need to give a copy of the forms indicated to the doctors and nurses. Also, you'll need to call us when the baby is born and we'll communicate further with the hospital and inform the baby's adoptive parents."

"The instructions are inside then?"

"Yes. There is a checklist inside with detailed step by step instructions on how to proceed after you reach the hospital. You will also need to return here one more time after leaving the hospital to sign the final adoption papers."

"What is this?" Mom almost interrupted the end of his sentence, seemingly having found something in the packet.

"Ah yes, I almost forgot about that. That is a request by the new parents. Because they do not know you or how you're interacting with the baby thus far and clearly cannot do so themselves, they've asked me to pass this book along to you. Don't fret about it too much. It's a simple request that you can ignore if you wish. They won't know either way. The mother wanted me to request that you read a story or two from the book."

"Read a story to the child?"

"Oh yes, babies are wonderfully responsive to our voices while in the womb. It would not surprise me if yours was listening to our conversation right now."

Not withstanding the eerily accurate presumptions of Doctor Weaver, I was still trying to ignore much of what they said. The details of the new parents rattled inside my brain endlessly, refusing to leave. Even when I set to focusing on more appreciated memories, those of Heaven and my friends from before, I had no luck.

Not being able to ignore those thoughts was frustrating and I continually sought some means with which to distract myself. So, I floated sideways and back again, upside down and back again, then strummed by umbilical cord like a guitar for a few minutes.

Before I knew it, the meeting ended and my parents made their drive home. After settling in, they finally said something I considered important and of great interest.

"Do you really want to do this? He said we didn't have to." Dad commented.

"I know, but I just… I don't feel like we've done much."

"What do you mean? We've done everything, and we've done it all perfectly."

"That's not what I mean. I mean the little things. The things that normal couples do when they are pregnant; the shopping, the reading, the baby showers." Mom offered.

"I just don't want to see you upset, hun. I can't imagine what it must feel like."

"I'm sure you have an idea, Donald. It's your baby, too."

"It's…nevermind. It doesn't matter. What about this book though? Do you want to read or should I?"

"You're okay with this then?"

"I guess this other couple has been through a bit to get this far. It can't hurt to honor one simple request."

"Okay, I'll read first." Mom agreed.

They had never spoken to me before directly. Sure, Dad had spoken at me before and Mom had taken to her humming while sitting and resting, but I had never been addressed as a person, as a fellow human being. I ended every thought and movement that could be a distraction and listened, truly listened to the story and their voices.

"Willem von Eden saw many adventures in his days. He woke every morning to find a new villager or maiden at his door begging him to rescue their stolen goods or defeat a group of bandits. He never turned down a sincere request and so he never rested.

Willem enjoyed his travels immensely and had no desire to rest. For him, life was not worth living if it was not spent experiencing new things. Such was the reason that, at the rising age of 35 he had yet to settle down with a family of his own.

That is not to say that Willem did not fawn over the children of each and every village he entered, handing to them trinkets from far off lands, purple and rose stones polished to a brilliant sheen in which the children could see their faces. Any village which had seen Willem at least once before would pull out every stop when he arrived, preparing for him a feast on which he could have spent days.

This was the life of Willem von Eden, that is until the day on which a certain woman came upon him, dressed entirely in rags, a welt surrounding her right eye. "Great Willem! I beg of you your assistance. I have searched far and wide asking everyone I know for the greatest adventurer in the land. They all said your name."

"Peace and well wishes kind woman. What troubles you so?" He answered her kindly, but kept a sharp eye on her movements as he was unsure of her face. She did not display the face of sincerity. Hers was a face of shadows, of darkness and secrets.

"My child. I have lost my child. You must help me retrieve her." She wrung her hands and pulled at her hair the same as any woman who had lost her child, but her eyes remained sharp and calculating. Not a single tear lighted her cheeks.

"Be calm my dear. Come in and tell me more of your child." For some reason, he was not quite sure of, Willem invited the woman in. He supposed it must be from habit. Yet, inside she came and to him she relayed the entirety of her story.

Six nights prior, she had been traveling between Kingston and Bristol with her daughter in tow. The two had a single mule weighed down with too much baggage to carry one of them, so they both walked.

Two hours before going to sleep a band of robbers approached them. They did not speak, nor did they touch the mule. They simply grabbed the young girl, whose name the woman would not relay, and threw the woman to the ground.

Willem's heart was immediately drawn to the story. He

could not imagine such a horrid crime taking place in his home country and so, despite his misgivings about the woman, he assented to help her. She did not smile nor did she cry when she left, she merely bowed and thanked him.

The following day, Willem set forth for Bristol, having completely forgotten his misgivings over the woman in the rags. Instead, he focused on the poor young girl who had been kidnapped. Not long into his trip though, as he passed the boundaries of Bristol, he stumbled upon a pond.

The pond was silver – not just the silver of water that has not been disturbed in years, but the silver of an expensive serving spoon from a Duke's kitchen. He stared in disbelief as it shimmered, when suddenly it revealed the form of a man...or what Willem assumed was a man. The creature rose from the silver pond with a sheet of white light around its shoulders that slowly unfolded. They were wings and they drowned out even the light of the sun.

"Be still good sir. I have come to you to help."

"Are you an...angel?"

"As you call me, yes I am. I have little time though. You must hurry. The woman who visited you last night has cast a spell upon you. You seek a young girl, yes?"

"Yes, it is her daughter. She sent me to retrieve her from bandits."

144

WOMB CHILD

"There are no bandits. This woman seeks to steal the child of another."

"How could she?..."

"She is an evil woman, one who seeks to force others to give away their children for favors of dark magic. Everything she does is wicked."

"Then why does she need me?"

"Because a woman has forsaken her offer, refusing to bring her child to the woman in rags as was promised. She cannot take the child by force, so she must deceive another."

"And I am that man."

"You are."

"So, I'll just go back, find her and tell her no."

"You cannot now. You must go to the woman in Bristol and speak to her, warn her of the woman in rags and her plots. You must then protect her from future attempts to take her child."

Willem almost asked why it must fall to him to protect the child, but looking upon the angel before him, he could not ask the question. He knew that it must be this way. Somehow he just knew.

"And one more thing you must remember, Willem von Eden. You are still under the rag woman's spell. You will feel the urge to betray the child and her mother. You will feel the desire to give yourself over to that spell and take the child, but don't give *in. Once you have not done so in a month, she will come looking for you. You must be prepared for her to come."*

"I understand."

"Then I will leave you."

"Wait...How do I know that I will be strong enough to defeat the works of the evil one?"

"You will know. Just remember to watch and pray.""

The irony of the story was not lost on me, but I listened, enthralled by the tale of a child and his angelic protectors. It reminded me so much of the years I had spent in Heaven, wishing I could go below and speak on behalf of my friends, telling their parents what must be done.

The story was so compelling. I wanted to know what happened next, which made me realize that Mom had stopped reading.

"This is an interesting story. Who wrote it?" Dad asked.

"There's no author on the cover. It just says, *Tales for Children.*"

"It sure is an interesting selection for an infant. I wonder where they found it."

"I'm not sure...it hits a bit close to home though, don't you think."

"I was thinking the same thing." Dad said, "Are there any

other stories in there?"

"There are a few. I'm interested to see how this one ends though."

"I can keep reading if you like."

"I think we've read enough for now. Maybe I'll finish reading it later tonight before bed."

"Sounds like a good plan."

"For now, I'm feeling a little hungry."

"I can agree with that."

Though they had apparently decided not to read anymore to me that evening, I had the feeling that I would be hearing a lot more stories from the book. I looked forward to hearing the rest of Willem's story. Would the girl be kept safe with her mother or would the Woman in Rags steal her away? It bothered me to think that a girl could grow up not knowing her true parents, that she could so easily be taken. It bothered me even more to think that I would be facing the same situation.

Why would my future adoptive parents send Mom and Dad a book with such stories?

In the coming weeks, Mom would read to me each and every evening, choosing a new story from *Tales for Children*. She never finished Willem's story though. As I heard tales of Trolls living in cars, trees walking the sides of mountains and fairy princesses bartering with each other, I was both enthralled by each new tale yet impatient to hear the final parts of Willem's story.

Regardless of which story she told though, Mom's lilting voice kept me in rapture for half of an hour every evening. The last people I ever wanted to see after birth were the ad executive and school board member that Mom and Dad would allow to raise me. However, I silently thanked them for the *Tales for Children* that brought us together every evening.

Chapter 13

38 1/2 Weeks

Time was just about up. I could tell I only had a short while until it was time to leave. For days, I had been turned down in to the proper position, waiting for the next step in the process. This is something I was told about from the beginning.

My instructions for the most part dealt with the role I would play in making peace in the Middle East, but they also included what should be expected prior to my imminent birth. Certain things start to move; certain changes take place and I have already started experiencing a few of them.

Only two nights ago, Mom bolted upright, awake and in pain. Her pulse quickened and breathing soon followed as the first of many false contractions occurred, preparing her for my arrival. I knew it wasn't the final notice, but the panic it instilled in her bled through to me, and I surely only made it worse with an unintentional kick.

It's been awhile since I kicked for the sake of garnering attention. That's not to say I have given up. I now spend my days plotting, trying to craft a plan that will somehow get me out of here and into my mother's arms. I've heard time and time again the plans that have been laid out for me after I arrive, the quick evacuation from my Mom's hospital room to a separate location where my "new parents" will arrive to take me home.

The only conclusion I've been able to come to on a consistent basis is that I really can't do much from the womb. I muse often that if I still had angelic powers at my disposal, things would be a lot easier. Perhaps, I could just poke and prod a little bit more at their hearts. Somewhere in there was the answer too, somewhere in the heart. I just needed to know how and where to poke.

***

Today, morning came like any other and the daily routine persisted. Dad had already left for work and Mom was methodically brushing her teeth, something that had become much nosier recently as her belly grew closer to the source of the rushing water each day. For some reason, she took a lot longer than usual. This wore on my patience because I wanted for her to hurry and eat. I seemed to be hungry constantly these days, never quite full. I maneuvered the fully formed thumb on my left hand to my mouth in anticipation of whatever nutrient rich breakfast she might put together today and the orange juice that would immediately follow.

She never ate nor drank the orange juice though. She never showered, nor did anything else that would have been normal to us. Because, in the middle of brushing her teeth, the water still crashing wildly into the sink, I felt a sudden powerful release of pressure that seemed almost nonexistent until that moment.

Mom's water had just broken.

My heart beating rapidly, I checked my position. I was still upside down in darkness feeling the gravitational pull of the Earth like never before. It would be an easy birth, if her body was truly ready. Too bad the false contractions had only come two or three times; she may have been better prepared.

None of that mattered now as Mom realized what was happening.

"Oh...oh, Okay." She stammered in disbelief at first but promptly stopped. Moments later I heard the monotone dial of the kitchen phone. "Donald. Honey, I think it's time.

"Yes, the baby's coming.

"How long would that take?

"No, I'll drive. It's not far.

"No, I think I can make it. I'll meet you there?

"I love you too. Hurry, please."

Mom was regulating her breath now, slowly breathing in

and out, and trying to remain calm as her body prepared to grant me my freedom. I felt the contractions around me slowly start and stop. There was a lot of time between them and Mom needed all of that time to get to the hospital. I remained as still as possible, hoping to keep the pressure off of her long enough to get there.

I had witnessed the births of numerous children from Heaven over the years, choosing to watch the arrivals of those to whom I was closest. The urgent rush of energy expended by both mother and father; the panic of trying to manage time when everything seemed to be happening at once; the slow onset of labor pains unlike anything classes and books could have prepared the mothers for; all of these things were missing and yet here I was, a few short inches away from birth and the next level of life….and what seemed like the wrong destiny.

I quickly lost track of time as the gravity of the situation encompassed me. I was about to be born. Everything I had worked for over the years, all of the instructions I had received and all of the time I had spent observing came down to this one moment, a moment that was only hours or even minutes away.

***

The hospital sounded just like I remembered from above. The crisp, clean voice of a nurse announced pages and phone calls in an annoying echo. Chirps and whistles surrounded me, each one marking another life in the hands of these professionals. I heard Dad's voice only seconds after entering the heart of the hospital, calling out to Mom urgently.

Dad played his part well, barking questions to anyone who would listen, demanding special attention for his wife. He spoke softly to Mom, as though too much noise might startle me into arriving too soon. I was much too busy with my own preparations to do that. These were the final moments. I had repeated my instructions again and again in my head, along with a hundred thousand other things I had gathered in the womb. I wanted to remember Jeremiah and Rose's stories, Cecile and Adele's games of hide and seek, and Mom's fairy tale book, but most of all I wanted to remember my Mom and Dad. The people who had kept me safe and healthy for eight and a half months now, who I had spent years getting to know, even if they had no idea who I was, I still wanted to remember them. Because even if I never saw them again, maybe, just maybe, memories of them could help me remember my purpose in life. Maybe, I would be able to continue and complete the journey on which I had been sent.

Mom remained calm all throughout the chaotic experience. Dad asked her the questions for hospital admissions. A sweet, tender female voice asked her questions about contractions, which Mom happily answered with rather precise numbers. Ultimately, the noise of a dozen other men, women and children complaining of broken arms, twisted ankles and rattling coughs died down and I felt the relaxation in Mom's muscles.

Finally, they admitted Mom into a room and gave her instructions about changing into a gown. After shuffling around for a few minutes, probably dressing in her new hospital fashion, she settled in on the bed.

Before Mom could get too comfortable, a familiar voice arrived within our proximity. It was Doctor Sprigg. His elastic tone beat a path through the hospital room and welcomed us. "Mrs. Hillman. How are we doing this morning?"

"Besides the mind numbing contractions every five or ten minutes, just great."

"Completely normal, my dear. With the health of you and the baby so far, it wouldn't surprise me if he was born within the hour."

"I hope so."

"Yes… looks like the excitement has started."

"Excitement? I wouldn't call it that. There is nothing exciting about pain."

"So have you thought about something to help you through this? Epidural, maybe?"

"No," Mom winced, "I want to go natural."

"No need for heroics, so if you change your mind please

let us know. But if you wait too late, you'll have to go it alone. Either way, I'm sure you'll be fine. Childbirth is such a magical experience. Even after all of these years, I still marvel at it." He spoke in a sing song voice as though he were reading from my story book.

"Doctor Sprigg, we're giving up the child...for adoption." Mom's admission sounded as full of guilt as I had always wanted it to and yet the pain in her voice hurt so much. I had never quite understood these strange people that were supposed to be my parents, but I loved them nonetheless.

"Oh, I am sorry, my dear. I did not realize."

"No, it's okay. I never mentioned it," Mom said, "I think I might have been trying to ignore what was happening." The last part was spoken softly, in the same voice she read to me with, so I presumed she was speaking only for my ears.

"I am sorry. I must converse with the nurse for a minute. I will send Donald in momentarily. I passed him at the desk on the way in, but he should be finishing up now."

"Thank you, Doctor Sprigg."

Although, I was a little jaded about my parents focusing primarily on their finances and very little on me, I could never hold anything against this couple who had been chosen to raise me and even now I held out the smallest sliver of hope that something might change.

Again, I wondered how possible it really was for me to remember anything after birth. If so many others before me had failed, why would I succeed now? After all, look how easy it was for my parents to forget one of their major assignments- to raise, nurture, and cultivate the child who would one day save the world from mass destruction. I wanted so badly to help them remember, but now was definitely not the time. The nurse just checked my mother's progress, poked me in the head in the process and told her to start pushing.

In the final moments, I felt the muscles surrounding my lower body tighten and those near my upper body relax. The contractions were doing their job hastily. A wail of pain screeched from my mother that almost sent us both over the edge. I still managed to repeat and pray about everything I wanted to retain after I was born.

'*I was destined to be born and raised a Hillman. I had spent much of my time in Heaven as an angel bringing together, my birth parents, Carrie and Donald Hillman. They were meant to be together. I spent years ensuring their happy union and even now, amidst the torrid upheaval of their lives, they continue to love each other. And it is love and the lack of provisions that caused them to seek a better life for me through adoption.*

Even with different parents, I pray that I will remember the nobility of my purpose, that I will grow up with the conviction in my heart that my role in life is important. Much as Cecile had overcome the turbulent waters of youth, I pray that I will remember and do the same. Please let my adoption enhance my life, not hinder it.

The world needs me more than it could possibly know. I overcame the threat of return, of being cast away from earth by my parents. I will also overcome this final barrier and grow into the man I was destined to become. I will remember and perform my purpose- to negotiate peace between the nations of the Middle East. I will eradicate the promise and possibility of a major nuclear uprising. This is vital.

And finally, I pray that my Spirit stays connected to God who will always cause the vicissitudes of life to work out for my greatest good.'

Immediately, I felt a peace that passes all understanding and knew it would all work out. I then clearly understood, "it is finished". My story had already been written, it was up to me to walk it out, no matter what.

Chapter 14

38 1/2 Weeks and Some Minutes

All at once, the world exploded in a violent burst of color. The light was blinding, a sharp, piercing jab in the back of my head. My ears rang with the aftershock of Mom's screams, still carrying through the room. The two men hollered from either direction, trying to help, offering advice.

Finally, with an ear rending scream and a twist in my spine so violent I thought my head might pop off, two meaty paws yanked me free. It felt as though a powerful fist punched me in the gut as air rushed into my lungs, erupting in a throaty cry that I hadn't realized was in me. I felt the ebb and flow of rushing air viciously climbing its way in and out of my lungs as the blur of light continued to rush in and out of focus. I had seen nothing but darkness for eight and a half long months and the sensation of active sight was so foreign that I could not remember quite how much I was supposed to see.

Still crying, still sucking in air and squinting against the explosion of fluorescent light across the ceiling, the room continued to swim. *Doctor Sprigg* swiveled my body around, moving me awkwardly in funny little circles as he said things I couldn't quite make out.

Suddenly it hit me. *Doctor Sprigg.* I remembered his name, the crisp single syllable I had grown so accustomed to over the months. That meant, Mom and Dad! I remembered Mom and Dad! I didn't know how long my memory would last though. No one had ever been able to tell me how long it would last after the birth. It could be days, it could be minutes.

I began to bellow, "Mom, Dad! Don't get rid of me. It's me, your son." I said whatever I could think to make them change their minds, as loud as I could.

"Is the baby okay?" I couldn't see Mom through the haze. Everything around me was a discolored haze, everything except for the pink-shirted nurse to whom the doctor had handed me off.

"His crying is quite normal. He's just stretching his lungs a little bit. I'd be more worried if he were silent."

"*He*? Did you say '*he*'?" asked the misshapen blobs that were my mother and father.

A simple "yes", is all the nurse offered.

There were dozens of blots in my vision, blurry spots that I couldn't be sure actually existed. The dark colors of their hair in disarray, my father leaned towards Mom. It looked like he might be holding her hand.

I cried again and again to them, hoping to make them look at me.

"We'll clean him up for you and bring him right back."

"Actually, we've filed adoption papers, so, we'd rather not. Here are the forms you need." Dad said it matter-of-factly while Mom remained silent. I tried to watch them, to see what was on their faces, but my eyesight was still underdeveloped. Still, the appearance of even their hair and arms attached to the floating anomalies of their bodies made my heartstrings sing.

"Sure. Well, I'll send along an orderly with the rest of your paperwork then. Doctor Sprigg will return shortly to check in on you, Mrs. Hillman."

"Thank you." It sounded as though Mom might cry, the tender quiver in her voice I knew so well. And then she was gone.

The nurse had me in her arms, cradling me gently within a swath of blue cloth. For so long I had floated in the confines of the fluid filled sac within my mother. The space around me now was immense. I cuddled as close to the nurse's arms as I could and continued to cry for my Mom and Dad. They had to have heard me.

I continued to wail, even as the pink shirted nurse placed me into the softest cushion I had ever experienced, something I immediately realized was the *only* soft cushion I had ever experienced. The nurse brushed her delicate hand against my cheek and stepped aside. The conflicting elation of birth, of those first few moments of life and the pain of my parents waving me away like a broken vase fought for dominance in my heart. I continued to beg, to ask for the nurse to return. I needed to see my parents, to look into their eyes. I could convince them that I was theirs, that I belonged in that room with them.

It is impossible to describe how it feels to finally awaken for the first time with the power of sight in a human body. I couldn't help but wonder if anyone was watching me from above, observing my journey and waiting along with me to see what would happen. I didn't care, though. I didn't care what the others above thought or what Jeremiah would have done. I just wanted to see my parents, at least one last time. So I continued yelling, demanding I be taken back.

Finally, from the corner of my eye I saw a floating bubble of yellow round the corner above my soft cradle bed. Another nurse, one who had stood and watched as I cried, indifferent the whole time, spoke to the one who had laid me down. "One of the orderlies told Mrs. Hillman that her baby was crying a lot and she changed her mind about seeing him. Why didn't she want to see him before?" She said, her confusion evident.

"Adoption."

"Oh."

"Yeah. Well, time to go break her heart a little more,"

she replied just before wiping me up, placing some icky drops in my eyes, slapping a tight cap on my head and a loose garment on my body, with me yelling through the entire process.

The pink-shirted nurse lifted me free from the cushions and walked down the hallway. I blinked many times, hoping to clear my eyes enough to see Mom and Dad when I arrived. Trust is hard to come by after so much betrayal though, so I continued to cry even louder, begging to be taken to my parents, demanding to speak with them.

Hoping it was not a trick.

"Mrs. Hillman. Mr. Hillman. I have your son." The pink shirted nurse rounded another corner and entered an open door. The hazy clouds of color, my parents, near the far wall jerked in response. I couldn't make out their faces or their bodies, but their voices were so familiar, the only thing I had known for the last 8 and a half months.

"Oh, Donald..." Mom exclaimed.

As the nurse took me closer to them, I saw my opportunity. Mom's face came into focus at last, a peach-shaped frame, pale and smooth, mottled with sweat and the remnants of her ordeal only minutes before. Her hair was in a tangled mess above her head and tears settled in the corners of her eyes then trailed to the edges of her mouth. Her lip quivered once and I immediately stopped my yelling.

162

WOMB CHILD

Looking into her eyes, into the face of my mother, I saw a woman of great beauty and intellect, torn by so many conflicting emotions that even she was not sure how she felt at the moment.

I realized that I no longer felt as she did nor moved where she moved. Yet, as she took me into her arms, the familiar comfort of being close to her heart took hold and I snuggled as close as I could to her, burrowing into the tangled sheet and green gown she wore loosely over her shoulders.

Even as she began to cry ever so softly, I closed my eyes and pushed closer to her skin, hoping that if I were close enough, she might feel what I felt and understand what only I knew. When I reopened my eyes, Dad was staring down at me, as well, his head pressed gently against Mom's. His hair was on end, ridiculously out of form. Each of his slightly oversized ears was a pale red, contrasting the tan complexion on the rest of his face. Tears streaked his cheeks. In all of my months within Mom I had never heard him cry.

Both Mom and Dad looked as though they had been through war. Their tears were flowing freely now. I tried to cuddle back against her, but she held me slightly away and started shaking her head. Dad rubbed the small of her back twice and started to walk away.

"I'll get the nurse. I might as well make the call while I'm out here."

"Okay." Mom pushed the word through her lips with great difficulty, then caressed the inside of my supple hand with her own.

The pain in her face was clear but I could not bear to be taken away again. I knew right then why she was supposed to be my mother. Doing the only thing I could think to do, I gripped her finger in my right hand, holding tightly and pulling it towards me, hoping she would pull me back towards her.

"Mom. You probably can't understand what I'm saying to you right now. You have to know though that I belong with you and Dad. You are meant to be my parents. Nothing matters anymore. I don't care about the past; the adoption, the clinic. It doesn't matter. I need you to take me home and raise me as your son because there is no other woman on this planet who can do it like you."

To my ears, the words resonated on two levels. My angelic senses still picked up the meaning, even as they slowly faded within my Earthly body. However, my human ears, those tiny wafer-shaped attachments, registered the soft, melodious tone of an infant's coo.

I knew that Mom could not understand my words, but still I gripped her finger, holding it tighter still to my chest as she stared into my face. I kept speaking and watched. Slowly, the puckered corners of her mouth began to rise, a smile forming gradually in the ruins of tears and exhaustion.

At last, she pulled me close to her and held me against her chest as tightly as she dared. "I won't let them have you. Do you hear me?"

And I did hear her. With the same elation I had felt moments before, seeing her face for the first time, I knew I was in the arms of a woman who loved me. We remained like that for what seemed like an eternity, but was likely only a few short minutes.

Dad's voice captured her attention. "I made the call. Greg is on his way down."

Mom's face was ashen. She looked back at me deeply then at Dad again. A moment later, the nurse returned and started towards us. I began to squirm. A reminder of my fate settled over me like a funeral shroud, blackening everything I saw as I realized this woman was going to take me away again. *Mom don't let this happen.*

The pink-shirted nurse tenderly removed me from my mother's arms, clearly trying not to look Mom in her weeping eyes. The nurse turned, walked halfway out of the room, and I started my vocal protest once more. No matter whose ears listened, they heard an honest, guttural wail that rivaled any city's emergency management system.

"Call him back. Tell him never mind." Mom said it triumphantly, as though she had finally won a hard fought battle.

The nurse turned back towards my parents, now too far away for me to see clearly any more. I started whimpering. No longer was I yelling or pleading.

"Carrie, hun. What are you saying?"

"I'm saying, we're keeping him. I don't care about Greg. This is *my* son."

Dad's heavy hand rested lightly on my stomach, slowly pulling me away from the nurse and into his sturdy arms. He ran his hand over my covered head and returned me to Mom.

Dad's smile came much quicker than Mom's. He kissed her softly and poked my stomach more delicately than I could have expected with such a massive finger, "This *is our* son."

"His name is… Israel." Mom said it as though the word had suddenly appeared in her mind, perhaps a final vestige of my angelic gift, my last spark of influence before the fullness of my humanity enveloped me.

The pink-shirted nurse brought her face close to mine so that I could see the filmy green centers of her eyes, "Israel, huh? Oh look, he must like his name, he's smiling." She commented then continued, "and what a wonderful name you've chosen for such a beautiful baby. It means, *Prince of God*. I have no doubt that he will do great things."

WOMB CHILD

I'm sure you're right, I thought. If only I can remember…remember… *What was I supposed to be remembering?*

Discussion Questions

1. What did you enjoy/dislike about this book?

2. Is it realistic to believe that problems in life create layers that often get people off their course to achieving their greatest potential?

3. What specific themes did the author emphasize throughout the novel? What do you think she is trying to get across to the reader?

4. What did you appreciate the most about Israel's character?

5. Did Carrie's mother do the right thing by not convincing Carrie to keep the baby? Could she have been a greater influence?

6. What do you think Israel's parents could have done differently? When should they have done it?

7. What do you think of Jeremiah?

8. Do you think Jeremiah ever remembered his purpose?

9. What emotion best describes how you felt at the end of the novel?

10. Do you know or suspect what your life's purpose is?

About The Author

Alethea Pascascio is the author of two critically acclaimed titles, *Bag Lady* (a story of forgiveness) and *Help Wanted: A Woman's Guide To Strategically Position Men In Her Life.* She is a much sought after speaker for topics on forgiveness and relationships.

Currently, Ms. Pascascio is busy on her next book and the screenplay for her title, *Bag Lady.*

To contact the Author about this title and others or to schedule a speaking engagement- send email to:

Alethea@queenpublications.com